THE AUTHOR

Diane Marshall was born in a tenement flat in Johnstone Renfrewshire and started her writing career by completing a number of short stories.

She went on to write a play called 'The Attendants' that was staged in the Mitchell Theatre Glasgow. The play was performed by an all-star cast and she was hailed as 'one of the finest writing talents to emerge in Scotland for years' by The Scotsman in August 2003.

Her first novel 'Beyond the Light' followed soon afterwards and now she has completed her first Historical Novel.

Based in Scotland it is a story of love, betrayal, and a secret that changes the lives of many of the characters in the novel especially Maggie Brown.

http://www.shieldcrest.co.uk/diane_marshall.html

The Curse of Baird Hall

By

Diane Marshall

© Copyright 2012 Diane Marshall

All rights reserved

This book shall not, by way of trade or otherwise, be lent, re-sold, hired out, or otherwise circulated without the prior consent of the copyright holder or the publisher in any form of binding or cover other than that in which it is published and without a similar condition including this condition being imposed on the subsequent purchaser.

ISBN 978-1-907629-38-9

MMXII

Published by
ShieldCrest
Aylesbury, Buckinghamshire, HP22 5RR
England
www.shieldcrest.co.uk

For my wonderful grandson,
Oliver Thomas Barnes
From Nanny Scotland

Many thanks to my friend
Duncan Brown, Artist/Piper, for
creating the cover for my book.
www.handpict.co.uk

≈ 1 ≈

She ran as fast as her legs could carry her across the front field, with her skirts pulled up as far as her knees. Tears of frustration blurred her vision as she lost her footing and fell down on the hard, uneven ground. Scooping up the bottle of laudanum that had flown from her hand, she pressed it tightly to her breast like a precious child.

'Please, God, don't let my mammy die!' she cried aloud as she scrambled to her feet and ran on. The wind swirled and danced around her face, making her lose her breath and still she ran... her heart pounding, fit to burst.

Three-quarters of a mile away in a small tied cottage, lay her mother. Exhausted with the effort of breathing, she gulped at the air like a drowning soul. 'Oh Maggie, hurry, lass,' she gasped, 'there are things I need to say to you before I meet my maker, and, please God, forgive me for my sins… especially the one that will be so hard for her heart to take.'

Lizzie Brown knew that she was near the end of her life; a life that had not been easy, despite what the village folks said. A gossiping lot they were and no-one knew it more than herself. And they had gossiped, and not only that but they had made life so hard for her that if it hadn't been for her beautiful child, she knew that her dying day would not have waited this long to catch up with her. Oh, but she had loved and been loved in return, and made to feel like a queen; a cherished, adored queen. Tears sprang to her eyes as she thought of him, away from her and unable to tell her that everything would be alright. She didn't want him to be sad. All she wanted was for him to look out for their daughter, Maggie; her pride and joy.

The wind blew open the small window above her bed and the cool air swept in like a welcome friend. She drank it in, smelling its sweetness. As she lay looking up at the sky through the window, she longed to see the trees once more but, as she tried to focus, her eyes dimmed and the window seemed to slide away from the wall.

She gulped at the air with great gasps, and then suddenly all pain left her and she smiled, welcoming the serenity that swept through her body and mind like a warm calming tide. Her eyes that were still fixed to the window space grew dim and, instead of the window, there came into her view the face of her daughter, her sweet smiling Maggie. She closed her eyes and quietly slipped away.

Maggie could see the cottage from the brow of the hill and relief flooded through her veins, spurring her on. The nearer she got to her home, the faster she was able to run. She loosened the ribbons of her bonnet and let it fall to the ground as she reached the kitchen door.

'I'm here, Mammy!' she cried, still holding on tightly to the bottle of medicine that Mrs McCaw from the village had given her earlier. She threw off her shawl and made to go straight into the small square living room where her mother had spent the last three weeks on the bed near the fire, close enough to the window to enable her to see the sky.

She hesitated before entering the room. With one hand on her heaving breast, she tried to slow her breath that was running like the Puffing Billy. She knew that something was wrong, for her mother would always greet her in her usual manner by saying, 'Hello, my bonny lassie.' But the silence hung heavy in the air like a grey cloud.

Her shoulders dropped as she looked at the medicine in her trembling hand and then she slowly peered around the door. Her mother lay as still as night and Maggie ran into the room and threw herself across the bed. As she looked at the face of her mother, still beautiful in spite of the harshness of life, she whispered, 'Oh Mammy, Mammy.' Then her tears fell like rain and dripped onto her mother's silent breast.

It had become dark outside when Maggie heard the tap on the kitchen door, and Katy Baxter – her only friend – swept into the room like a breath of fresh air. But she stopped short and cupped her hand across her mouth as she realised that Mrs Brown was dead. 'Oh, Maggie, I don't know what to say… I am sorry for you, really I am.'

'What can you say?' the heartbroken girl replied. 'My mammy's dead and that's an end to it.' Katy tried to persuade her friend to come away from the cottage and spend the night in the village with her family, but Maggie refused to leave her mother's bedside. Eventually Katy left to fetch Mrs McCaw, the village midwife, and the one called to lay out the dead before the undertakers took the unfortunate soul on its last journey. And she supposed that at this time in the evening, she would most likely find her three sheets to the wind.

As she trudged the three miles to the village, her thoughts were not entirely with her bereaved friend. Instead they were full of fantasies about Robert Turner. Just the thought of him could put her head in a spin and no matter what, Katy was going to get him. She thought back to the first time she saw him when she arrived at school for the very first time, clutching Maggie's hand and already afraid of Miss Bryson, the teacher, who loomed over them like a dark shadow.

And there was Robert; a year ahead of them and proudly marching along the cold corridor with his head held high, defying any teacher to mess with him. Of course, he wasn't much to look at back then, with his ill-fitting clothes and his big cousin's hand-me-down boots, two sizes too big for his feet. But there was something about him that made her smile and giggle for no reason at all whenever he was near.

Through the years she watched him grow into a tall handsome man, whose muscular body filled her with a longing the likes of which she had never known. Gone was the dirty-faced little character whose thick wavy hair was always falling into his eyes. She had seen him only yesterday while he worked on his father's farm, fixing in posts in readiness for a new fence. But he never noticed her.

'You could do a lot worse than him,' her mother had often told her and she knew that it was true. He was doing well and there was nothing he didn't know about farming. 'Once his father goes, he'll inherit a very good going concern. What with their cheese and milk output, you'd be set for life, girl,' her mother had told her.

But she had spoiled herself with Alec Scott and a few other lads from the village, if the truth were known, and no decent lad would take on a used woman… so he must never know the truth about her exploits. She quickened her step and pulled her shawl tighter around her shoulders as the night air began to bite.

Once she arrived at her destination on the south side of the village, she was relieved to hear the familiar chatter of several drinking cronies of Mrs McCaw's, spilling out from the open kitchen window.

As she announced her arrival by tapping loudly on the door, all went quiet for a second before Annie McCaw called out, 'What's up?'

'It's Katy Baxter… Mrs Brown has died and needs seeing to.'

'Come in with yea, lass. So she's finally given up the ghost, has she? Well, it was only a matter of time. The last time I saw her she looked like the finger of death had already marked her.'

Katy could detect the heavy smell of stale ale in the air as she walked into the kitchen and quickly made her way to the range to warm herself by the fire. Around the table sat Mabel Forrester, Jeannie Cummings and Mary Fields, the biggest gossips in the village.

'Well, if I'm not at the birthing, I'm at the other bloody end,' complained Annie McCaw. 'I never get a minute's peace these days. They're going out as fast as they're coming in. When did she pop?'

'Sometime this afternoon, as far as I can tell,' said Katy.

'This afternoon? Oh, for Christ's sake, she'll be as stiff as a bloody board and what the hell can I do with that? Well, I'll be charging a penny or two over my usual rate for the inconvenience. I'm sick telling them to get a hold of me as soon as they go, not hours bloody later. It's just as well that I'm a charitable woman when all's said and done. Still, now that you're here, you might as well help yourself to a drop of ale. Fetch a jug from the chest and sit yourself down while I get Jack to set up the old cuddy and trap.'

As Katy sat sipping her ale, she felt sure that Maggie would be mortified if she could see her with a jug in her hand. Still, it was none of her business, and she was quite partial to a drop of the stuff from time to time.

'Well, I wonder what Miss High-and-Mighty will do with herself now that the old yin has bitten the dust,' said Mabel.

'Aye, she'll know all about it when the Laird puts her out on her fancy breeks, that's for sure. Pampered wee madam that she is.'

'You're bloody joking!' cried Mary Fields. 'Take it from me, that old bugger up there has a soft spot for the girl. I wouldn't be surprised if he weren't bedding her.'

'Well, who could blame him?' said Jeannie. 'Have you seen his Mrs at close range lately? It's enough to turn milk sour.'

The women laughed as they sat around the table exchanging knowing glances and Katy wondered if there could be a ring of truth to their suggestion. After all, Mrs Brown did seem to have a good relationship with the Laird, and her widowed at that.

'Well, come on then, let's get this over and done with,' said Annie as she came back in to the kitchen. 'Our Jack's all set to take us.'

Katy sprang up from the table and set her bonnet straight and smoothed down her skirts as she followed Mrs McCaw outside. 'Mind and leave some ale for me when I get back, you greedy shower of buggers,' she called on their way out.

Jack McCaw was the apple of his mother's eye and, even if he wanted to, he would never be able to get lost in a crowd because of his shock of carrot red curly hair that earned him the nickname of Rory Rid. He stood by the side of the horse with a grin on his freckled face and, as they passed, he slapped Katy on the backside. In return she playfully slapped him on the arm.

As they trundled along, Mrs McCaw started to snore and Katy sat red-faced at the memories of the previous Friday night in the stable with Jack.

≈ 2 ≈

The servants were buzzing like bees as they sat around the white scrubbed table in the kitchen of Baird Hall. Each and every one of them had something to say about the funeral the day before.

'It's a good job the Laird is away on business, or else Madam Brown would be out on her ear by now.'

'Don't be so bloody daft, lassie,' said the cook. 'It's not him that she needs to worry about; the Mistress will have her out by the night, you mark my words. She won't wait till he comes all the way back from London. She hates the sight of the girl.'

'But where will she go, the poor thing?' piped up young Jessie Kirk, much to everyone's surprise, for she was a girl of very few words.

'She can do what she wants as far as I'm concerned, as long as she doesn't come knocking on my door,' said the parlour maid.

'Aye, you're just scared in case that man of yours takes a shine to her, that's all,' said Mary.

'Shut it, the lot of you,' interrupted Cook, 'and get on with your breakfast before I set the lot of you to work without any.'

Without saying another word, they started their meal of porridge with chunks of bread and large pitchers of creamy milk.

Robert Turner had taken the wild flowers his mother had given him, and made his way to the cemetery behind the Kirk in the village.

'After all,' she had told him, 'that poor woman never had a chance in this village, and all because her husband died before her bairn ever saw the light of day. It's a wonder she never lost it, the way the villagers carried on. Still, cottage or no, she worked her fingers to the bone to dress that madam up at the big house. Aye, she more than paid her way alright.'

The Kirk sat on an incline almost three-quarters way into the village and it had been the place where Robert had worshipped not only the Lord, but Maggie Brown. For as long as he could remember he would anxiously wait in the pew beside his mother and father Sunday after Sunday, just to get a glimpse of her. And in she'd come with her mother, who would be smiling almost proudly by her side, as if to say to the world, 'Yes, we have a right to be here.'

How she would cope without her mother's strength worried him to the point of distraction.

As he rounded Reek Street and passed by the creaky old disused barn, he had made up his mind that once things had settled down, he was going to ask Maggie to the winter dance.

On reaching the Kirk, he walked round toward the graveyard and stopped dead in his tracks when he saw her standing there with her head bowed. Her chestnut hair glinted in the sunlight; simply tied back at the nape of her neck beneath her bonnet, it tumbled down her back. Her already slender form looked to be smaller somehow as she stood dressed in her jet mourning clothes.

For a moment he wondered if he should leave her be, not wanting to intrude in her thoughts. But just then she turned and saw him standing there looking rather awkward. And, as always when he caught sight of her beautiful face, his head went into a spin and all sense seemed to desert him, and when she smiled, he was lost…

'Robert,' she said with a note of surprise in her voice. 'How are you?' she enquired.

Finally managing to get his feet into motion, he walked toward her and said, 'I'm a lot better than you must be at the present time. I… Well, I came to pay my respects. Oh, and my mother sent these,' he said, handing her the flowers.

'That was very kind of her. You will thank her for me, won't you?'

'Oh aye, I'll do that, Maggie.' He was standing close to her now and he noted how tired she looked.

'How are you managing?'

'I'm alright most of the time, it's just that I miss her so badly…' As tears welled up in her eyes, he took her in his arms and held her close. He wanted to tell her how he felt and that he would never leave her, but instead he let her cry and felt a pain in the back of his throat that threatened his own tears.

Katy had caught a glimpse of Robert passing by earlier, as she leaned over into the window of her father's confectionery shop to fetch a slate of treacle. Seeing him with the flowers, she knew that he would be making for the graveyard. She couldn't wait to get rid of her customer, and the minute the young boy left the shop she tore off her apron and ran to catch up with Robert.

She watched him and Maggie from her hiding place behind a tall, weather-beaten headstone and she was furious; even more so when they left together and headed out of the graveyard the back way, toward the clearing that ran parallel to the woodland. She had always known that there was something special about Maggie, for she had the ability to turn most men's heads. But not only that, there was something about her that drew people to her, wanting to hear what she had to say with her soft voice and expressive eyes.

'Well, Maggie Brown, you're not getting him, I can promise you that. And, friend or not, I would rather see you lying next to your mother before I let you take the only chance I have to better myself.'

Baird Hall was a seventeenth century tower house that sat majestically on a hill, overlooking the Ayrshire lowlands. Its square central tower could be seen for miles around and was revered for its splendour. Malcolm Baird's ancestors had commissioned an extension to the property in the year 1721; it was since then that the hall was said to have been cursed. And for the last hundred and fifty years mothers told stories to their children on dark winter nights of the terrible goings on at the Hall.

The curse was said to have been brought to the Hall after Eliza Duncan married Henry Baird in 1721; Malcolm's great-great-grandfather. The ambitious young bride oversaw the extension to the Hall and had particular interest in providing an elaborate nursery wing, complete with utility room, school room and ample quarters for nannies, teachers and servants. Throughout the considerable time that it took for the work to be completed, Eliza and Henry were dismayed that there was still no sign of the children that they so wanted.

It was not until she had reached her thirtieth year that she found that at last she was with child. There were great celebrations at the Hall and, in order to spread the good news, a great party was thrown in honour of the coming event. But there were whispers amongst the servants at the Hall that the Lady was too old to give birth to a healthy heir, and it was said that she had begun to act in the strangest of ways.

The Curse of Baird Hall

From the start the pregnancy had been difficult, and during that long, bleak winter Eliza was confined to her bed. On the night of the birth there had been a snowfall that had started the previous afternoon and never let up for the rest of the night. Eliza's labour had started the previous morning, and the attending midwife was said to have left the agonized woman for far too long before she sent for the doctor.

By the time his exhausted horse had pulled his buggy through the snow and finally reached the Hall, it was too late for him to save the child. The story goes that the midwife ran screaming from the birthing room as soon as the infant was born, leaving it to die between its mother's legs. When Eliza saw the child, she cursed the midwife and all who would give birth in the future at Baird Hall, for her child was born without a face.

Throughout the remainder of that terrible night and into the next day, all that could be heard were the agonized screams of the demented mother before she died with the dreadful curse on her lips.

The heartbroken Laird left the Hall and did not return for three years until finally he brought a new bride to the Hall. Having met Catherine Howard, the daughter of a wealthy mining lord at a ball hosted by Lady Victoria Lewis, cousin to the Howards, he fell in love with her and they soon became inseparable.

They were married amongst the splendour of Catherine's home in London and when they returned to Baird Hall she was already five months pregnant. The terrible tale of his first wife and the death of his child did not deter the young bride, although they did make a pact to leave the Hall well before her confinement.

And so every heir born to the Baird family thereafter was neither conceived, nor born at the Hall. However, the lineage was not without its problems and it was said that Malcolm

Baird was born prematurely at the Hall, condemning him to a childless marriage. Although he married young, there was a great scandal at the time as his wife, Regina, was a widow and had a two-year-old boy who was named William.

The marriage had been far from happy and servants at the Hall heard frequent battles between the two for the first two years of their union, and now, eighteen years later, they barely spoke. Long gone were the huge parties that once lit up the Hall like a Christmas tree. So, too, dwindled the dinner parties that were renowned for their excellence. Regina Baird earned her reputation as being a very malicious woman, whose treatment of the household staff was so bad that she once beat a parlour maid till she bled.

The Hall's substantial employees halved in numbers shortly after the new bride arrived and were replaced by handpicked staff from her own choosing. Many villagers felt heart-sorry for the Master, for he was a fair man both in business and in deed, and why he chose that woman for his wife was a source of never-ending wonder.

It had been four days since Maggie's mother had died and the day she had dreaded was now upon her as she walked the dirt path that led to the drive of the Hall. Her mind was in a swirl. When the message boy appeared with the instructions for her to report to Lady Baird herself, she became flustered and had dressed in a hurry.

She wished with all her heart that the Laird had returned from his business trip and would at least be about the Hall somewhere. But she knew in her heart that if he had come back, then he would have called on her to offer his condolences.

She was to report to the servants' entrance at the back of the house by 9:30 sharp, and it had just passed 9:20 when she rang the doorbell. It seemed to take ages for someone to answer the door and she shivered in the cool September breeze.

When the door opened, there stood Jessie Kirk – a short, pale-faced girl that Maggie knew from the village. She had always liked Jessie, but now they smiled awkwardly at each other. Maggie had never seen Jessie dressed in her uniform, which was a grey working dress overlaid with a white starched apron. Her frilly cap looked to be at least two sizes too big and, as she beckoned Maggie in, she scratched the top of her head, moving the cap sideways.

'Well, I've just been told to leave you here till I go and fetch Mrs. Mead,' she said, before adding in a hushed tone, 'I'm that sorry to hear about your ma, Maggie, and my da is an' all.' Then she disappeared through a door.

As she waited, Maggie looked around the small square entrance which had two doors leading off; one on her right and the other on the wall facing her. There was a plain stone stairway on the left and the steps were worn in the middle through booted feet tramping on them over the years. There was also a musty smell to the area, as though something wet had been left lying around for days.

Suddenly the door facing her opened and she got such a fright that she jumped. The woman standing in the doorway looked Maggie up and down and raised her left eyebrow in a rather disapproving manner.

'What's the matter with you, girl?' the woman enquired. And, without waiting for an answer, she said, 'Get inside, will you! I can't be doing with ditherers.' As the woman stepped aside, she informed Maggie that she was the housekeeper and would be addressed as Mrs. Mead.

Maggie followed her into the room and watched as the woman seated herself behind a large desk. She had seen her in the village Kirk many times before, but being this close to her was quite intimidating. She was slightly built, with steel grey hair tied neatly in a bun at the nape of her neck. Her face was long and thin and her nose looked as though it had once been broken, for it had a large bump in the middle and the whole appearance seemed too long for a face to carry.

As Maggie stood in front of the desk, the woman shuffled through some papers that were lying on top of a battered old leather writing wallet. She studied the housekeeper's face closely and saw that it was heavily lined, and had two deep indents on her forehead giving the appearance of a permanent frown.

'Well,' the housekeeper said finally, 'with your mother's passing, you are no longer a tenant at Thistle Cottage and you will leave immediately. I have a paper that you will make your mark upon and then you will leave.'

Shocked, Maggie stood staring at the woman whose lips showed just a hint of a smile whilst her narrow eyes had all but disappeared as she screwed them up in a malicious manner.

'Well, girl, are you going to stand there all day with your mouth open?'

'But the Master had made arrangement with my mother…'

'Well, the Master changed his mind,' interrupted Mrs. Mead.

'But I don't understand!' cried Maggie.

'What is there for you to understand? The Master wrote out this document and had it witnessed by his solicitor, which clearly states that under no circumstances were you, Margaret Maria Brown, to remain in the cottage following the demise of your mother. If you were educated, I would give you the document to read yourself…'

'Oh, but I am educated, Mrs. Mead, and if you don't mind I would like to read the document for myself.'

Somewhat taken aback, the housekeeper handed Maggie the paper, and sure enough, the script told the same sorry story. She fought back tears as she gazed at the document, but she was determined not to give this vicious woman the satisfaction of seeing her cry.

Her heart was pounding as she walked closer to the desk and laid the paper down flat on its surface, lifted the nibbed quill and signed the document, then shook sand across her name. She looked into the eyes of the housekeeper, and in a steady voice she bid her good day and left the room.

Back in the small square reception room, she almost fell over Jessie who had been listening outside the door and heard every word.

Jessie Kirk was considered to be the lowest of all the household servants, as she worked as the laundry maid and did not live in. She had started her employ at the Hall three years previously at the age of thirteen, and before that she had nursed her sick mother until she died. Her father was the well known village drunk, who spent most of his time either sobering up or getting drunk.

She stood and watched Maggie Brown as she walked along the drive from the Hall, with her head held high and her step firm. Jessie had been under strict instructions from Cook to listen at the housekeeper's door and report to her straight afterwards. As she walked into the kitchen, a sea of enquiring faces sat staring at her from around the large wooden table.

'Well?' asked Cook.

'I couldn't hear much,' she lied.

'Oh, for God's sake!' cried one of the kitchen maids. 'I knew it was a mistake to send her, she's bloody useless.'

'Oh, get back to the drying room before I cuff your lug for you,' said the cook, her disapproving tone sending Jessie scurrying from the room. 'She's a brainless piece and that's for sure,' she added.

When Maggie was far enough away from the Hall, she sat on a low dyke by the side of the dirt track, unable to hold her tears at bay any longer. She cried until she felt sick. She couldn't believe how Malcolm Baird had turned on her. Her emotions were torn between the love and respect she'd felt for the man, ever since she had been a bairn.

She had loved him as deeply as if he had been her own father and she felt bewildered by his change of heart. She was even convinced that the housekeeper had been lying, but the official stamp on the document told her that it was real; real and awful.

Robert was unable to concentrate on his fencing and decided that he had earned a break. He downed tools and headed across the south-facing field toward the farmhouse. His mother was busy in the kitchen rolling out dough on the marble-topped table that she used for baking. She looked up with a quizzical look on her face as Robert passed her, taking his work shirt off as he entered the small adjoining scullery.

After wiping her hands on her apron, she stood by the open door with her hands on her hips as she enquired, 'What are you up to coming in from the fields at this time in the morning?'

'You know, Ma, I can't remember the last time I had a break,' he said. 'So I'm taking the rest of the day off, and I might even have a few in The Starr Inn the night,' he winked cheekily at her.

'Oh, aye, that'll be a fine sight to see, I'm sure,' she said with the corner of her mouth lifting up in a smile.

As she watched her son ready himself, she couldn't help but feel proud that he had grown into a fine looking man with a fine strong body. She thought back almost twenty years to the morning he was born; a mere wee scrap of a thing so small and frail that she had feared for his health. And to look at him now, with his thick dark hair and his easy smile, she wondered how much longer he would get away with being single.

Half the lassies in the village were daft on him. But for all his strength, he had a sensitive side to him and had a heart as big as a turnip. She worried about his relationship with his father, for the two were like chalk and cheese, and the older Robert got, the more they quarrelled because Tom was hard on him.

When Robert came back into the kitchen, he was wearing his best cotton shirt and brown trousers.

'Aye, you'll do,' said his mother. And as he kissed her cheek, she said, 'Tell the lass I was asking for her.' He looked surprised for a second and then hugged her before he left.

The Lady of the Hall had made her appearance downstairs and had ordered tea for two in the drawing room. Mary Fields was nervously adding a small flower arrangement, set in an ornate silver bowl on a tray, whilst Cook placed scones onto a plate.

'What's up with you? You're dancing around there like you were ready to pee yourself,' said Cook.

'I don't mind waiting on her, though that's bad enough,' Mary replied. 'It's that son of hers that gives me the creeps, lazy bugger that he is.'

'Aye, he's worth the watching and that's for sure. He was sniffing around Mabel the other day and he's the sort that just takes what he fancies. Mind you, I don't think she would say no to him, being the Laird's son and all.'

'He's not even his son. If he was, then he'd be a nicer fellow,' said Mary. 'His real da could be a murderer, for all we know.'

'Aye, but he'll get the lot when they're gone, so best keep your opinions on that score to yourself or we'll be out on our back ends. Now, get that tray on the trolley and wheel it in there before she pulls that bloody bell.'

William Baird sat opposite his mother in the very comfortable drawing room of the Hall.

'Of course, you do realize,' he said, 'the consequences of your little… shall we say, fabrication of that document, don't you? When Father returns from London, I should think he would be just a little upset by your actions, to say the least!'

A light tap on the door silenced him and his mother shot him a warning glance. 'Come!' she said, still levelling her attention on her son.

'Your morning tea, Ma'am,' said Mary as she pushed the trolley into the room, taking great care not to splash any of the boiling contents of the teapot onto the lace cover. She positioned it by the side of an occasional table before proceeding to pour.

'Leave it!' said Regina Baird with such an impatient tone to her voice that Mary was only too happy to leave the pouring to them.

'Very well, Ma'am,' and with a slight curtsey she left the room, muttering under her breath, 'Crabbit old bitch.'

Smiling in a way that always infuriated her, William said, 'You really should be nicer to the servants, you know, Mother. One day they might all up and leave and then you'd have to make this wretched stuff yourself.' He pointed to the laden trolley.

'And that would never do, would it?' said Regina. As she got up from the couch and walked over to the trolley, she added, 'You would not be able to take your pick of them, would you?'

'My dear mother, it is my right as head of the household…'

'You're not head of anything yet, and don't you forget it.'

'Really, Mother, this conversation is beginning to bore me; could we just get to the point of this cosy little get-together? I really do have better things to do.'

'My God, you make me sick to my stomach! Do you realize the effort I have put in to secure your position? Not to mention the sacrifices I have made over the past eighteen years in this house, living with a man I can barely stand to look upon.'

'Well, Mother, that's what a loveless marriage does for you. Although, why you can't consider his feelings once in a while, leaves me quite confused. After all, he is rather a good provider.'

She studied her son with rising anger, her normally pale completion deepening as she digested his words. Oh, she knew exactly what he was like and didn't expect any more of him than he already was – cruel, selfish and greedy.

He had known since the age of sixteen that Malcolm Baird was not his father and that his mother had been a widow when they'd met at a social event in London hosted by the late Lady Finchray, then an ageing but powerful member of high society who had taken quite a shine to the young and pretty widow.

Once introduced to the mild-mannered Malcolm, the rest was easy for the one-time small part actress from the theatre in Drury Lane, who went by the name of Christina D' Loris. But her true acting ability far exceeded the small parts seen by London's theatregoers. Her best performance was played to the unsuspecting Malcolm, who was besotted by the pretty young widow who had supposedly been left penniless by her husband.

A sad picture was painted of the struggling young mother whose mine-owning husband had gambled away his entire empire before succumbing to consumption, leaving her with a two-year-old child. In truth, Regina was a clever calculating woman whose acting talents paid off in the end, when she snared Malcolm Baird. And the secrets she had strived to keep hidden were now threatening to expose her for what she really was, rather than the picture she had painted so well.

William stood to inherit the entire estate once Malcolm died, and to that end she never stopped plotting. And now the time had come to tell her son the truth about his real father. She regarded him now as he sat there with his legs spread out in front of him.

Still dressed in his riding clothes with his arms folded across his chest, he looked every inch the country gentleman. He was a handsome fellow, no doubt about that; his dark blond hair made him appear younger than his twenty years. But it was his piercing blue eyes that were the spitting image of his natural father, and as the years passed so too were his mannerisms.

A tap on the door snatched their attention away from the matter in hand and, without waiting to be bid to enter, the housekeeper walked into the room.

'Ah, Mrs. Mead,' said William as he rose to his feet. 'I expect you have household business to discuss with my mother. I was just going in any case, so I will leave you to it.' As he reached the door, he turned toward his mother and said, 'I won't be home for dinner tonight, Mother.'

Once he'd gone, Jean Mead knew that she had interrupted them before Regina had had a chance to reveal the whole truth to him.

'For God's sake, Jean!' snapped Regina. 'Didn't I tell you to give me enough time to tell him before you came in.'

'Yes, but I thought you would be finished by now.'

'Well I wasn't. I hadn't even started. Not that he was interested, all he wanted to do it seems was to get out as quickly as possible. You just gave him the excuse he needed.' Regina looked at her sister and added, 'How many years have we been planning and plotting and skulking around this house, pretending that we are employer and employee, with him never knowing the true state of affairs? He must know soon before anything happens.'

'Don't fret yourself,' said Jean as she helped herself to a scone and poured some tea. 'He'll know soon enough and, believe me, when he does he'll be in on the plan, of that we can be sure.'

Maggie had no idea how long she sat on the dyke as she tried to quiet the turmoil that kept rising up and running through her like the swell of the tide. She thought down through the years of her childhood living in Thistle Cottage with her mother. She could see her now in her mind's eye, as plain as day, sitting at the long narrow sewing table stitching the latest fashions for the Baird family.

She had sat by the side of her mother who was determined that Maggie would never enter into service at the Hall. And so she had learned her mother's craft as an accomplished seamstress. The work paid for the rent and also gave them enough to ensure that they had a reasonable standard of living.

So why Malcolm Baird was now so eager to evict her from the cottage, she could not comprehend. She thought that at least she would have been asked to carry on as seamstress to the Hall, but the cold and seemingly indifferent way that she was being treated now left her reeling. All she remembered of Malcolm Baird was a very nice gentleman who seemed to be truly interested in their wellbeing. His visits to the cottage…

Her mind stopped dead, as she said out loud, 'His visits to the cottage!' Suddenly she sat bolt upright. 'Oh my God, Mother, no!'

Covering her mouth with one hand and steadying herself on the dyke with the other, the sudden realization of what was bombarding her mind threatened to take the legs from under her. She slowly slid down the side of the dyke and slumped onto the damp undergrowth as her mind reeled in disbelief.

And as she faced the fact that she could never remember him visiting during the daylight hours, her heart hardened against him. Hatred flooded through her veins as she bit hard onto her knuckle, drawing blood as she strived not to scream.

≈ 3 ≈

Robert's heart pounded as he neared Thistle Cottage, only to discover two carpet bags and Maggie's furniture strewn across the small front garden. Once he got closer, he heard voices coming from inside.

'The bastards have thrown her out,' he said aloud as he quickened his step toward the door, which opened as soon as he stepped foot on the front step.

'Who the hell are you?' asked the rough-looking woman who stood defiantly in the doorway.

'I was just going to ask you the same question, Mrs.'

'We're the new tenants and I would get that lot,' she pointed to Maggie's possessions, 'to hell out of our garden.'

Just then a man appeared at the door. 'Who is it?' he wanted to know.

'Robert Turner, that's who. And I want to know where Miss Brown is?'

'Oh, Miss Brown, is it? That's a different name for her,' said the man.

Robert could feel his anger rising and as he stepped closer to the unkempt man, he recognized him. He was none other than Alex Walsh from North-Bar, a small village two miles away; a no-good troublemaker who thought with his fists.

'And what do you mean by that?' replied Robert.

'I mean that she was his piece on the side and now…'

Before he could say another word, Robert punched him square on the nose, sending blood squirting out across the floor where the man landed flat on his back. The next minute Walsh's wife and their two daughters were on Robert's back, screaming and punching at him.

Just then Maggie had emerged from behind the high bushes at the end of the woodland and, as she neared the cottage, she heard the commotion and ran the last few yards to the gate. She stood transfixed. What was happening seemed to be taking place in slow motion, as she watched Robert wrestling the women off his back.

By this time Walsh was back on his feet and took a swing at Robert, catching him on the side of his jaw.

Maggie screamed and ran through the gate. 'Robert, what's going on? Who is this man?' As though she had just doused them all in cold water, the fighting stopped and they turned around to look at her.

'Maggie!' Robert called as he walked and put a protective arm around her shoulder. 'Come away, lass. It won't do any good to stay around here.'

'Aye, he's right there. Away yea go before I hit him again!' shouted Walsh.

'I'd like to see you try,' said Robert as he picked up the two carpet bags from the damp grass.

'Oh, I'll do better than that, boy,' shouted Walsh, 'for the next time, you won't even see me coming.'

Ignoring the threat, Robert guided the tearful Maggie out of the gate and along the dirt track. As soon as they were far enough down the track, Robert dumped the bags down on the ground and made Maggie sit down on top of them. When she was seated and looked up at him with her tear-filled eyes, his heart melted and he struggled with his feelings. All he wanted to do was to hold her in his arms and never let go.

'I can't believe that those people are in my home. How could they do this? After all the years my mother spent working her fingers to the bone for them.'

'It serves no purpose for you to tear yourself apart wondering about the whys and wherefores, lass. Who are we to understand the minds of the gentry? They're a cold-hearted bunch and that's for sure, but I'll tell you this, Maggie Brown, there's not one of them in that house fit to clean your boots.'

She looked into his eyes and was so aware of the sincerity they held that she laid her head on his chest and was comforted by how good it felt.

'Now, you're coming with me,' he said as he helped her to her feet.

'But where can I go?' she asked him as he hitched the bags onto his shoulder.

'Home with me,' he replied as he caught hold of her hand and held it firmly.

They walked in silence toward Shields Farm and all manner of thoughts were running through Maggie's mind. How could she stay in the same house as him, feeling the way she did? And as the shock of the morning's events began to wear off, the sudden terror of being homeless and without a job sank in. She had never in the whole of her life felt so desolate.

'For the umpteenth time, the boy deserves a break,' said Ina Turner as she stood in the kitchen with Robert's father, Tom.

'What the hell is he thinking, running off the way he did with not even a word?'

Ina watched her husband as he stood gazing out of the window and, not for the first time in their marriage, she felt like slapping some sense into him.

'Oh, for God's sake, drink your tea and eat your piece before the lassies come in from the dairy and run right out again at the sight of your face, so red it's fit to burst.'

'Aye, that may be, but I'll have a few choice words for that lad when he gets in the night,' said Tom as he took the mug of steaming hot tea and walked out into the courtyard.

Robert and Maggie had just reached the hoolet pass and from there they could see Shields Farm down in the valley below. Maggie slowed her pace and looked out over the fields and her heart sank.

'What's the matter?' asked Robert. 'I can't just turn up at your house in this state. What will your mammy say?'

'Well, she might start with hello,' he said, a cheeky grin lighting up his face.

'Oh, you!' she playfully pushed him and, for the first time in a week, she smiled.

A serious expression crossed his face as he said, 'For God's sake, lass, you've just lost your ma and been chucked out of your home, don't you think you're entitled to be in a state?'

'I know what everyone talks about in the village and around here. They think that my mammy, and myself for that matter, were doing more for the Laird and his son than sewing.'

Robert swung around and grabbed her by the shoulders, his face pale with anger. 'I never want to hear you say that again, Maggie Brown. What do they know? Nothing, that's what. And what they don't know, they'll not be slow in making up.'

Surprised by the fervour in his voice, she hung her head onto her chest and once again gave way to her tears.

'Aw, don't cry, lass, they're just jealous and that's all there is to it, now come on.' Once again he took her by the hand, only this time she clasped onto his tighter.

One of the dairy maids had just left the kitchen and was headed back to work when she saw Robert's familiar figure walking across the north field with a lassie. Turning back toward the farmhouse, she called out, 'Looks like you've got visitors, Mrs. Turner.'

Ina came to the door to see what all the noise was about and as soon as she saw Robert with Maggie Brown, she quickly closed the kitchen door and turned to the dairy maid and said, 'Go on now, girl, get back to work.'

She walked toward her son, noticing the red scuff on the side of his face. 'Oh my God, what's happened?' she asked.

'Now, Ma, don't get all worked up.'

'Oh, she's not the one that's worked up, boy,' interrupted his father, who had seen them coming. 'And what the hell is she doing here?' he added as he looked at the carpet bags.

'She's been evicted from the cottage and has nowhere to go...'

'Oh, so you thought you'd just bring her here, is that it?'

'Aye, that's it,' answered Robert vehemently.

Before he could say any more, Maggie leaned her body up against his before falling to the ground.

'Oh my God, she's fainted clean away!' cried Ina. 'Get her away inside.'

Robert picked her up from the flagstones and was surprised at how light she felt in his arms. Hitching her up closer so that her head rested on his shoulder, he walked past his father with a look of defiance in his eyes and took her indoors.

Katy was just closing up the shop when Annie McCaw appeared at the door.

'Oh, lass, I'm that glad I caught you before yea shut. Only if he doesn't get his liquorish sticks tae shove in his gob the night, my life won't be worth living.'

'Aye right then, Annie, come on in before anybody else sees you. They might think I'm working bloody overtime.'

As Katy tied the usual amount of six of the black sticky sweets together, Annie said, 'Have you heard about your crony from Thistle Cottage?'

'What about her?' she asked.

'Well, she's only been chucked out, bag and baggage, and a new family has already moved in.'

Katy stopped what she was doing and gazed at Annie. 'When did this happen?' she asked.

'This morning, as I heard it. And that's not all,' the woman eagerly continued. 'The minute that Robert Turner heard about it, he rushed away from the farm and went to collect her himself. And I got that from none other than one of the milkmaids from the Shields.' She finished relating the story with a satisfied nod of her head.

Katy rounded the counter and thrust the liquorish sticks into Annie's hand and led her to the door. 'I have to go,' she cried as she pushed the surprised woman out onto the street and locked the door.

A bemused Annie stood outside the door and peered in through the glass to see Katy running into the back shop, taking her apron off as she fled. Oh well, she thought as she turned and headed for home, if she thinks I'm paying for these the next time I'm in her shop, she can think again.

Katy was furious! And as she ran through the scullery, her surprised mother informed her that her tea was on the table.

'I'm not hungry. I have to get up to Shields Farm. Maggie's been evicted and was taken to the Turners'.'

Nelly Baxter could not help but gawp at her daughter's back as she ran into the front room.

'Where's my blue bonnet?' she screamed.

'Well, it won't be in here. And what's your hurry, anyway?' her mother asked.

'Oh, you wouldn't understand,' she said impatiently as she ran out the front door, leaving her mother standing in the lobby.

≈ 4 ≈

Malcolm Baird sat in a hansom cab as it trundled its way through the streets of London. Wiping the tears from his face, the words of his friend and solicitor Edmond Lloyd were still ringing in his ears… 'She died a week ago.'

'My Lizzie is dead!' he said aloud, as the cab slowed to a crawl whilst negotiating its way through a crowded narrow street.

To the right of the cab he saw a barefoot street urchin steal a loaf of bread from a trader's stall and quickly hand it over to a passing accomplice, before darting into the throng and disappearing with their meal. He felt sorry for the boy, who looked to be about eight years old, poverty-stricken and undernourished. He wondered what would become of him.

Thoughts of his own daughter flooded his mind, and a panic rose in him that took his breath away. But he quieted himself with the knowledge that, though she would be broken-hearted, at least she was safe in a comfortable home.

How would she receive the news that he was her father? The plan that he and Lizzie had made to tell her together when he returned from London, was now left to him alone. Could he convince her that her mother's relationship with him had been one of pure love? For theirs was love; wholly and complete.

As the cab left the dirty streets behind on its way to Portman Square, Malcolm felt the weariness settle into his bones, whilst his mind plagued him with punishing thoughts of Regina. For the millionth time since he brought her home to Baird Hall, he asked himself the same question yet again. Why did he marry her?

Yes, she had been beautiful and bewitching, but their whirlwind romance and quick marriage had now left him half the man that he once was. Edmond's words rang through his ears, reminding him that he could not divorce Regina, for she had been clever enough to convince the outside world that she was a devoted wife.

In reality, the truth was that she was nothing more than a cold and calculating woman, hellbent on securing the Baird family fortunes for herself and her spineless son. It all hadn't seemed so bad when he and his Lizzie would talk of their future together in front of the cosy fire in the cottage, while their daughter slept soundly in the bedroom.

Dear Lizzie, who had wanted nothing more than his love and refused vehemently on several occasions to move into the spectacular Hill View House, two miles east of the Hall. Still it lay empty, its only occupants being the housekeeper, old Cathy, and her caretaker husband, George, making sure that the house was kept warm and clean.

The view from the cab had changed and instead of the dirty crowded streets, the horse trotted along Oxford Street and then turned into Portman Street.

Once past Portman Square, they turned left into Berkley Street. The driver jumped down and pulled out the step. 'That's you, governor,' he said cheerily.

With a weary sigh, Malcolm stepped down onto the street. He looked up at his sister's house, and it was such a welcome sight that he felt his throat tighten with emotion. He quickly paid the cabbie, lest the man should see the tears that were threatening.

Under the bell by the side of the door, the brightly polished nameplate simply read, C. M. Fenwick. He managed a smile and thought at long last she had changed the nameplate; she had been widowed for the past ten years.

To his complete surprise Connie answered the door herself and, upon seeing his rather sad expression, she threw herself into his arms.

'Oh, my dear, you look terribly unwell. What on earth is the matter?' And as she closed the door, the man who had been following Malcolm turned up the collar of his greatcoat before turning around and making his way back along the street to where his cab waited.

Thomas Macey was no handsome sight; he was short in height and lean with it. His face was long and haggard and his right eye dragged downwards at the outer corner, with a thick scar running back toward his ear. It was a reminder left from an attempt to do away with him three years earlier. He had lived all his life in London, begging on the streets as a child until the age of nine when he had become a skilled pickpocket.

Born in a basement in Dorset Street in Whitechapel to an alcoholic mother, his father had been well known as one of the most skilled robbers in London. And they had lived from day to day either in famine or feast, depending on his father's spoils.

He had known Regina Baird as a barefoot urchin running through the streets of London. But she had a head on her shoulders and a lust for the good life; so much so that she groomed herself into a fine lady whose stolen clothes made the picture complete.

Securing herself a post in service at the age of nine, she learned the skills needed to pass herself off as a lady. And, by

God, she pulled it off. Her short acting career followed that and by the time she met Malcolm, she was confident in her role. Posing as a young widow with her infant son, she and the boy finally snared the unsuspecting Malcolm Baird.

As he was one of the richest land owners in Scotland, she was well pleased with herself and he was pulled in hook, line and sinker. Now fed up with playing the Lady of the Manor, the greedy bitch wanted the whole lot for herself and that brat of hers.

Not that he minded bumping off her old man. Macey was getting paid handsomely for his trouble, but he couldn't help wondering what she would do if her son's father appeared back on the scene. That would throw the cat among the pigeons for sure. The thought appealed to his menacing nature and he was smiling when he entered the Ten Bells pub.

The air hung heavy with chimney smoke, tobacco and the smell of stale ale, and it was full to the brim with prostitutes and local traders discussing the day's selling of their wares at the Spitalfields Market across the street. The market was new to the area and had only opened the year before, in 1887, making a handsome return for the pub's coffers.

Billy, the proprietor, looked up at Macey and nodded in the direction of a vacant seat which he took beside a roaring fire. A young girl he hadn't seen in the pub before, wearing a soiled apron, appeared by the side of the small table.

'What will it be?' she asked.

'I'll have some mutton pie and a pitcher of your finest ale,' he said, 'and be quick about it.'

The young girl stared at him for a few seconds longer than she had intended and he said, 'Well, don't just stand there with a gawk on. What the bloody hell are you staring at anyway? Less you think I'm Jack the Ripper?' he added menacingly.

The girl let out a yell and quickly darted over to the bar where she stood beside the burly proprietor, whose loud laughter started off the rest of the pub's occupants who had heard the remark.

'Bloody hell, girl!' shouted one of the local prostitutes who'd had one too many gins. 'Who the hell would approach him on the street? Not for ten bob, I wouldn't, and that's a fact.' There followed an uproar of laughter.

'Bloody women,' he said as he spat into the fire.

'Leave the young 'un be,' said old Ma Willis as she joined him at the table. She had known his mother when they were both young and pretty girls determined to run away together and make their fortunes overseas. But the life they were born into had imprisoned them in Whitechapel, and it was a fight for sheer survival as soon as they left their mother's breasts. Some managed to escape the poverty of the filthy overcrowded streets whilst others, like herself and her friend, were doomed from day one.

'You ought to watch what you're saying, Thomas Macey. It ain't right you making fun about The Ripper. Women are terrified here about and it's hard for them to make a bloody penny at the best of times, so you think on, lad,' she said as she turned to scan the crowd. 'Where the hell has George gone now?' She was referring to her drinking buddy.

'He's likely out back having a piss,' said Macey, 'but if he doesn't show his face by the time I'm finished me meal, I'll see you home alright.'

Ma Willis patted him on the hand and smiled her thanks as she left him to eat.

By the time they left the pub, the atmosphere on the dark streets was so tense that they could smell the fear. Still, they chatted about old times and Macey found himself telling her of his plans to get out of London once his latest job was done.

'Don't worry, Ma,' he told her. 'I'll make sure I send a shilling or two your way.'

As they made their way along Commercial Street and past Christchurch Spitalfields, Ma Willis quickened her step and clung on tightly to Macey's arm, keeping her head pressed into his shoulder until they reached The Britannia pub on the corner of Dorset Street.

A few minutes later, when she was safely settled indoors, Macey continued along the street to his ground floor rooms. He thought of the money he was set to get once he had murdered Malcolm Baird, and it excited him. Once indoors, he felt weary and settled down to sleep.

Malcolm and Connie, as he preferred to call her, had just finished their meal and retired to the drawing room. Sitting in front of the large cheery fire, his weariness began to settle in. Connie studied him as he sipped his brandy and her heart went out to him.

'The best thing we could do is to bring Maggie here,' she said. 'It's about time I got to know my niece. She would be introduced into the society that she was born to receive, and there are many eligible gentlemen of considerable means who would fall at her feet.'

Malcolm thought for a few moments before saying, 'Somehow I can't see her in London, enjoying the high life. She loves to walk through the fields and feel the wind in her hair, stopping to pick wild flowers, sitting beside the river watching the fish jump. And in winter, she adores the silence over the land that the snow brings.

'The long cosy nights spent reading by the firelight,' he stopped talking and searched back in his mind to only last winter when the snow had reached fifteen inches. 'How beautiful she looks by the firelight,' he said, his eyes glinting and his voice thick with emotion.

Feeling frustrated and totally helpless, Connie felt the anger rise in her chest and she wanted to scream.

'Darn and blast that woman!' she cried, her normally pale complexion turning a deep red. 'To think that you have put up with Regina all these years, not to mention William, is beyond human endurance. There must be some way that you can divorce her.'

'For what reason?' he asked, spreading his arms out from the sides of the chair. 'Lizzie is dead and I should never have listened to her when she begged me not to make our relationship known. I should have been strong enough to fight for the woman that I loved, instead of going along with the situation as it was.'

'You would have been ruined,' said Connie. 'The church would have cursed your union, not to mention your business contacts, and Regina would have been hailed as the wronged woman whose husband preferred the love of an employee of the Hall. And that is the harshest comment I will ever make of Lizzie.

'For, while we knew the situation, the world outside that little cottage would say exactly as I have. Maggie would never have stood a chance in society for she would be known as the bastard child of a union between master and servant and that is the reality of it. So don't tear yourself apart with regrets; your hands were well and truly tied.'

Malcolm stood up and said, 'I'm going to bed.'

Fearing that she had gone too far, Connie ran to catch up with her brother just as he reached the door. 'I'm sorry, Malcolm,' she said with tears in her eyes.

And, as she looked up into his face, she knew that she had been forgiven.

≈ 5 ≈

Robert Turner sat by the side of the couch and watched Maggie as she slept, his eyes taking in every detail of her face; the face that he had loved ever since they were children.

He chided himself for not having come clean with her years ago, but he was so afraid that she would reject him. God knows, she deserved so much more than he could ever give her. But his love was strong and true and if she could be happy settling for a dairy farmer, then his life would be complete.

He gazed at her thick dark lashes and her perfect mouth and he was overcome with a desire to kiss her. 'I'm going to tell you how I feel, Maggie,' he whispered.

Just then she moaned softly and in the quiet private world of her dreams, he was there and she was smiling up into his handsome face, content to lie in his arms. When the sleep left her, she opened her eyes… and felt confused for a second. Then the day's events blasted through her mind like a steam train.

'Easy, lass,' said Robert as she shot up to a sitting position.

'How long have I been asleep?' she asked.

'You've been out cold for a couple of hours, but that's only to be expected after the day you've had. Now the first thing we need to do is get some food inside you. Come on,' he said as he led her through to the kitchen where his mother was sitting at the white scrubbed table.

'How are you feeling, lass?' asked Ina as she stood up and made her way to the black leaded range.

'I do feel much better, thank you, Mrs. Turner.'

'Now you just call me Ina,' she said. 'And sit yourself down while I get you some food.'

As she ladled out a thick beef and vegetable stew, Maggie's mouth watered whilst Robert cut a thick wedge of bread and poured a steaming hot cup of tea. Halfway through the meal Tom came in from the dairy and the atmosphere immediately changed and became heavy with an uncomfortable silence.

'Do you want some tea?' asked Ina.

'I'll take nothing at that table till she's gone,' he said looking straight at Maggie.

In a flash Robert was on his feet. 'What the hell does that mean?'

His father rounded on him and, raising his voice, said, 'Everyone knows what she is. Not content with laying down with the Master at the Hall, now she thinks she's going to get her boots under my table. Well, it won't happen!'

He thumped his fist on the side cabinet. 'No wonder the Mistress waited till he was away on one of his London trips before she slung her out.'

Maggie jumped up from the table, accidentally knocking over her tea, and ran to the kitchen door. Meanwhile Robert had jumped up and grabbed his father by the lapel of his jacket and glared into his face.

'Aye, go on then, hit me if you think you can, boy. A bloody blind man could see the effect she has on you.'

'Stop it, for God's sake!' cried Ina, who ran to try and haul Robert away from his father.

At that moment they all turned toward the door as Katy's voice called above the commotion.

'I tried to knock, not that anybody in here would hear me. What's up with Maggie?' she asked, holding her friend in her arms as she sobbed.

Robert went to take hold of Maggie, but Katy pushed him away.

'Leave her be. She's coming home with me,' she said as they quickly left the room.

As Robert made to follow them, his father shouted, 'You follow her, boy, and it's the last time you'll ever see this house.'

Suddenly Ina broke down in tears, falling onto her knees in the middle of the kitchen. Appalled at the state of her, Robert lifted her up and sat her down beside the range.

'Ma, don't,' he pleaded, his voice quivering with emotion. He had only ever seen his mother cry once before and it tore him apart. With his arm around her shoulder, he looked over toward his father and for the first time in his life he knew hatred.

Katy was very pleased with herself as she and Maggie tramped over the back field toward the village. Even she couldn't have planned that sequence of events any better, for she thought that she'd have had the devil of a job persuading Maggie to come to live with her.

As it was, all had turned out well for the time being and she was surprised, not to mention delighted, to realize what Tom Turner really thought of the goings-on in Thistle Cottage. She had heard every word.

The next morning Maggie was up, washed and dressed before the rest of the house had stirred and, as she sat in the kitchen sipping tea, her mind kept rolling back to the night before. She suddenly realized that it wasn't so much what

Tom Turner thought of her that was bringing her down, but what Robert thought.

She wished she could see him now and feel his strong arms around her, keeping her safe. He had always held a special place in her heart but in the dimness of the early light, she realized that she loved him. And as the day broke and the light flooded the little room, so her heart lifted with the flush of love.

A noise from behind her startled her and she jumped up to see Katy's father enter the room, clad only in his nightshirt. An acute feeling of embarrassment flushed her cheeks as she averted her eyes from Hugh Baxter.

'Oh, don't be put off now, young Maggie. After all, we are living in the same house. Now, how about pouring me some of that tea you've got there,' he said.

And as he watched her, the longing in his loins quickened his breath as his eyes took in every inch of her. 'Don't worry, missy,' he thought silently. 'I'll be bedding you before the week's out. I'll give Malcolm Baird a run for his money.'

Aware that he was staring at her, Maggie was more than relieved to see Katy, still with sleep in her eyes, walk into the kitchen and plonk herself down at the table.

'Ta,' she simply said as she helped herself to Maggie's tea. 'I've been thinking...' she went on, 'seeing as how it's market day, you would be as well helping me in the front shop. Even though Ma sets up a stall down at the square, the shop still goes like a peerie.'

'Wherever I can lend a hand is fine by me,' said Maggie.

Before she could say any more, Hugh said, 'I think the lass would be better off staying this side of the shop the day, just till she gets settled in.'

'And do what?' asked Katy. 'No. She's better off in the front with me, at least that way she'll learn better. After all, she doesn't need teaching about housework. And anyway, it's Friday and wee Aggie always comes on a weekend to make the toffee and tablet and she does some housework, as well you know, so what's up with you this morning?' she asked her father.

'Too many women all in the one place first thing in the bloody morning,' he complained as he left the room.

The silence in the kitchen of Shields Farm was almost unbearable; both father and son had worked in the byres milking the herd, without one single word passing between them. And as they washed their hands before sitting down to eat breakfast, Ina fussed nervously over the porridge pot.

Robert stood by the cold press and drank a large mug of creamy milk and wiped the back of his hand across his mouth before he spoke to his mother.

'Don't put any out for me this morning, Ma. We've got a big order of cheese this week set for Glasgow. I'll away and get the cart loaded so that we can set off as soon as he fills his belly.'

With a quick peck on Ina's cheek he left them. And the silence returned once again.

The day was blustery and already the coldness blew down from the North, reminding chilled bones that winter was on its way. The sun that had dominated the sky early on settled behind a thick dark cloud and seemed determined to stay there.

When Tom came into the courtyard, the cart was all but filled to capacity. Before they set off, Robert retrieved Maggie's carpet bags that he had sat by the stone archway at the side of the dairy and put them onto the cart.

As they set off, Tom said, 'I'll deliver those to the Baxters' shop once we've sold this lot.'

'Like hell you will!' retorted Robert. 'I'll be taking them myself and you won't stop me.'

The village was swarming with traders and shoppers alike and as quick as they set up their stall, the cheeses were going like wildfire. Three hours later there was not a drop of milk or cheese to be had and, satisfied with the day's sales, Tom joined some of his cronies and headed for The Starr Inn.

'What's the matter, Robert?' shouted Alex Burns, who was reported to be so old that he had lost track of the years himself. 'You sickening for something, lad?' he shouted toward Robert.

'I'll be along in a bit,' he assured the old timer before he set off.

When he entered the shop, he had to wait in line until all the customers had been served. As he watched Maggie, he couldn't help but smile as she fumbled her way through a large order of toffee creams, tablet squares and toffee apples. When at last all was quiet, he handed her belongings over the counter but held tight to the handles of the bags.

'Can you get away for a while?' he asked.

'Well, you pick your moments, I must say,' piped up Katy. 'How can she get away with all this to contend with?' She spread her arms out behind the counter where there was a mountain of sugar, ties and bags littered over the entire work surface.

'It's simple,' answered Robert. 'She just walks out, and when we come back I'll gladly give you both a hand to clear up.'

Relieved to get a break, Maggie rounded the counter and joined Robert who said, 'Thanks Katy,' before they left the shop, leaving her fuming with anger.

As soon as they were alone, Maggie said, 'I'm so sorry for causing all that trouble last night, Robert, and if I could make it any easier for you and your mother then I would.'

'You are apologizing to me!' he said, astounded at the thought of it. 'Come on,' he said as he took her by the hand

and walked her swiftly toward the graveyard, where he led her into the shack that stood by the side of its entrance.

Taking hold of her by her shoulders, he said, 'I'm the one who should be saying sorry. My da had no right to say those things about you and I swear to God, if he or anyone else says anything against you I'll…'

'Don't,' she said as she put her fingers to his mouth. 'I don't want to bring strife into your life, Robert.'

His heart was beating fast as he looked into her eyes and he said, 'Maggie Brown, you bring nothing but beauty into my life and I love you.'

Tears sprang into her eyes as she moved closer to him and said, 'And I love you, Robert Turner.'

When their lips finally met, they were lost in the tenderness of the moment. He kissed her gently again and again and they clung to each other, enthralled in the wonder of their love. A commotion from outside startled them and they walked over to the crack in the door to see what the trouble was.

Robert was appalled to see his father fighting on the street.

'Come away, man!' cried one of the men from the Inn, as he dragged Tom away from the man he had knocked to the ground. Robert made to open the door when Maggie's grip on his sleeve stopped him.

'Please, don't,' she whispered. 'It would only make things ten times worse.'

It was over as quick as it had begun and, when the man on the ground stood up, Robert recognized him as Alex Walsh from Thistle Cottage.

'I might have known it,' he said, 'it's that idiot who moved into the cottage. He's had a good skinful by the looks of him and probably started shouting his big fat mouth off.'

He turned toward Maggie and held her close. 'Promise me that if you ever see him or any of his no-good family on the street, you'll get out of their way quick.'

'I promise,' she answered.

'I'll have to go and see what's up, Maggie, but meet me here tomorrow night.' He kissed her, made sure the coast was clear and they left the shack.

A few minutes later Robert arrived at the clearing at the centre of the village, only to realize that his father had left with the horse and cart.

'You took your time,' said Katy with a touch of anger in her voice.

'I'm sorry,' replied Maggie, a little shocked at her friend's attitude.

'Leave the lass alone, for God's sake, I helped you clear up so what's up with you?'

'Oh well, that makes everything all right then. My da decides to help me in the front shop, I'll put a notice in the window.'

'What the hell's going on in there?' shouted Katy's mother as she walked down the lobby and stood in the doorway, her hands on her hips. Hugh licked his finger and stuck it in a sherbet jar. 'And you get your hands out of there, you greedy pig. Well, I'm waiting…' she persisted.

'It's your bloody daughter, Nelly Baxter, if you must know, kicking off like a spooked horse and don't ask me what's wrong with her. You talk to her,' said Hugh as he pushed past his wife, muttering under his breath as he walked up the lobby.

'Have you two been arguing?' she asked Katy, whose face was so red it looked fit to burst.

'No,' was the short reply before she too flounced along the lobby.

With a sigh Nelly said, 'You might as well lock up in here and then set the table for tea.'

Alone in the front shop, Maggie fought back tears as she thought how peaceful and different her life had been in Thistle Cottage with her mother. And she wished with all her heart that she was back there.

The next morning was heralded in by agonizing screams booming up the stairs from the kitchen area.

Aggie Wallace, the weekend help, had gone into labour a month early and Nelly ran to the bottom of the stairs and shouted, 'Get your lazy arses out of bed and get down here! Aggie's bairn's coming!'

Hugh Baxter stood in the kitchen wearing his nightshirt and scratching his head as Nelly put some water on the range to boil.

'For Christ's sake, man, don't just stand there. Put your coat on and get Annie McCaw, and be quick about it.'

As he passed the bottom of the stairs, the girls almost knocked him flying as they rushed into the lobby.

As Maggie made to pass him, he grabbed hold of her and said, 'Easy on, lass, don't you know that bairns don't come flying out in five minutes? She'll be screaming till midnight.'

'Let go of me, Mr. Baxter,' said Maggie as she tried to wriggle out of his grip.

'Oh, Mr. Baxter, is it?' he said as he leaned closer to her. 'It's a shame that that bairn she's having won't have a fine pair like these to suck on,' he said as he cupped her breast in his hand.

Disgusted by the touch of him, Maggie drew her knee up and caught him in the groin, whereupon he immediately let go of her. She ran along the lobby and into the kitchen, relieved to be free of him. In that instant she made up her mind that she would not spend another night under his roof.

'Maggie, do you know if my da has left yet?' asked Katy. And, without waiting for an answer, she cried, 'I think it's coming! Help me get her onto the couch in the back room.'

As they struggled with Aggie, Nelly said, 'I'll go myself. That lazy swine will only be halfway up the stairs by now.' And with that she left them.

Ten minutes later she was back. 'That old bugger must have hit the booze hard last night, for if I threw a brick through the window and it hit her on the head, she'd still sleep through it.'

'Either that, or it would bloody kill her,' piped up Katy.

'Anyway, we've no time to think of that the now, Aggie's pushing. Quick, Maggie, hand me that towel and you'll find some shears on that block there,' said Nelly as she stuffed old newspapers under Aggie, who was screaming the place down. 'Mind and dip the shears in the boiling water, lass, and upstairs you'll find a shawl in the linen box by the side of the banister. Run and get it.'

Maggie hesitated. Her head was in complete turmoil, wondering if Katy's da was upstairs or by some miracle had gone out.

'Hurry, Maggie!' shouted Katy as the tortured Aggie screamed out again, only this time it sounded more agonized than the last.

Maggie jumped and took flight along the narrow lobby and headed straight up the stairs but, as she looked around for the linen box, Hugh Baxter was suddenly on top of her, knocking her to the floor.

She tried to scream but he held one hand across her mouth, and the weight of his body pinned her to the floor as he used his free hand to fumble with her undergarments. Her eyes were wide with fear, and unshed tears prevented her from seeing the lust in his eyes as he finally tore off her knickers.

The next instant his body weight swiftly lifted off her as though some unseen giant hand had picked him up.

'You dirty wee whore!' screamed Nelly as her husband hurriedly righted his nightshirt. 'What the hell is going on?' she demanded to know.

'I was just coming downstairs and she,' he pointed to the now sobbing Maggie, 'came into our room with her skirts held up to her waist.' He wiped his forearm across his sweating brow. 'She was begging for it. As I tried to get her downstairs, she took off her knickers and jumped up on me. I swear to God that's what happened Nelly, whatever the Master at the Hall taught her is below decency.'

Maggie could not stand listening to his complete pack of lies any longer and she threw herself at him, beating her fists against his chest, all the while screaming that he was a liar.

'That's it!' screamed Nelly. 'Get to hell out onto the street where you belong, you scheming wee trollop.'

She then hauled Maggie from her husband and pushed her. For a split second she teetered on the top step, and then went crashing down the length of the stairs, landing painfully at the bottom. She lay still for a few seconds, the wind completely knocked out of her.

'Oh, for Christ's sake, you've killed her!' said Hugh.

Just then Katy appeared at the foot of the stairs holding a squirming pink bundle wrapped in a bloody towel. 'What the hell!' she said, astonished at the sight of her friend lying there.

Suddenly Maggie moved and drew her legs up to her chest, then she sat up. With her head spinning, she crawled toward the front door.

'Maggie!' cried Katy.

'Leave her be,' said her mother as she ran down the stairs. 'Here, give me the bairn and you get her bags and get her on her way.'

'But Ma, what has happened?'

'Just do it!' replied Nelly as she walked into the back room with the crying infant in her arms.

An hour later, as they sat in the shack beside the graveyard, Maggie had related the whole sorry story to Katy. 'I'm sorry, Katy. I know he's your da, but he just went for me and that's the truth,' she finished.

Her friend was quiet for a few moments before saying, 'How could you say that about my da, Maggie Brown? After he opened up his home to you when you had nowhere else in this world to go. You are what they say in the village; you're nothing but a whore and you deserve all you get.'

With that Katy left the distraught girl sitting in the shack and ran back home.

Maggie sat there, shocked and in pain, and listened to the whistle of the cool autumn wind rushing through the cracks in the wooden structure that was her only shelter. She opened one of her bags and found a thick shawl and put it around her shoulders, then suddenly started to shake uncontrollably. But the tears that she needed to shed wouldn't come.

≈ 6 ≈

The streets of London were crowded to overflowing on this dull Saturday afternoon, and Macey sat in a hansom cab cursing the throngs as the driver fought for space. According to Regina, Malcolm Baird was due to leave London early Sunday morning, which would make his job impossible.

For two days now he had stalked the man without the slightest chance of doing away with him without being seen. 'Bugger it, man,' he thought, 'don't you ever go out without that bloody sister of yours?'

Tonight was his last chance, and if he couldn't get him on the street then he would have to find a way into that house.

Connie's maid, Millie Stevenson, had just delivered the afternoon tea into the plush conservatory. This was Connie's favourite room in the whole of the house, where she spent many hours reading.

'That will be all,' she said to her maid. 'I will see to it,' she smiled as she nodded toward the small silver teapot.

Millie smiled broadly at her employer, for never had she been treated so well in service and she was truly fond of her mistress. 'Yes, Ma'am,' she said cheerily before leaving the room.

'Well, would you look at this?' said Connie, holding the newspaper up in front of her. 'The Buffalo Bill Show has sold out again and has proved to be such a success that Queen Victoria has seen it three times!'

She lowered the paper and looked at her brother, who appeared to be lost in his own thoughts. 'Here,' she said as she stood by the trolley that was laden with freshly-made scones, potted meat and cucumber sandwiches, cream cakes and warm crumpets. 'Have some tea,' she urged.

'Oh, I'm sorry, dear,' he said, as though he had just awoken from a dream. 'What did you say?'

Connie studied her brother closely and, no matter how much she wished and fretted, it wouldn't change the fact that his inner turmoil was plain to see in his face and his eyes looked dead and empty.

'I'm concerned about you, Malcolm. Why don't you stay for another week? You haven't even begun to grieve yet, and if you go back to that woman in your present state then Lord only knows what will become of you.'

He thought for a moment before saying, 'Then why don't you come with me? It would make perfect sense.' He drew himself closer to the edge of his chair. 'We could both tell Maggie of her mother and I, and how impossible it was for us to make our union known.'

Connie looked thoughtful for a moment before saying, 'You know, I can't begin to imagine why I hadn't thought of that; it's the perfect solution. Of course I'll come. And once we finish our tea, I'll ring for Sam to get the carriage ready and then we will go shopping.'

'Shopping?'

'Of course, you silly old thing. Don't you want to take your daughter back something nice from London?' she asked. 'And I know the very place.'

For the first time since seeing her brother again, he smiled, and she felt a glimmer of hope return to her as she poured the tea.

Later, as the carriage trundled toward Oxford Street, they talked about a suitable gift for Maggie.

The sky had taken on a slate grey hue and a chill dominated the air as numerous carriages jostled for space through the busy streets.

When at last they reached their destination, it was already dark and a thick fog had settled in. Once inside the Mappin & Webb jewellery and silverware's impressive premises, all thoughts of the weather outside were forgotten as they browsed through the exquisite pieces on display.

Malcolm's attention was caught by a beautiful silver pendant, fashioned into the shape of a rose. When he asked to examine it further, he was enthralled to discover that the rose cleverly concealed a clasp that opened the piece up, and inside was hidden a tiny collar pin.

There were also solid silver drop earrings displaying a smaller version of the rose, and two hat pins with the tiny roses crafted onto the ends of them. To these Malcolm added a silver jewellery box, lined with royal blue velvet, which he knew to be Maggie's favourite colour.

'Oh, they are beautiful!' exclaimed Connie. 'Why don't you have the pendant engraved?'

Malcolm thought for a moment before saying, 'I think that's a splendid idea.'

A short time later, as they waited in an adjoining room whilst the work was being done, they drank tea and chatted about their forthcoming journey to Scotland.

'You do know that the weather back home will be considerably colder, so pack warm clothes,' he advised.

'Oh, don't be such an old fusspot,' she laughed. 'I'm not as delicate as I look, you know.'

Malcolm's eyes suddenly clouded and his smile vanished, only to be replaced by the haunted look that he had worn since attending Edmond Lloyd's office.

'What is it?' Connie asked.

'I was just thinking,' he said in a quiet tone. Then he added, 'Lizzie would never allow me to buy her anything and I could have given her so much. But she was so proud and insisted on earning her own living. "I will never be a kept woman, Malcolm Baird," she'd say.'

'But think of the love you gave her and the love she gave you... That is priceless, Malcolm. And whenever you think of her, remember those precious moments the two of you shared together and the beautiful child you made.'

A tap on the door silenced them as an assistant entered the room and announced that the engraving was complete. When they returned to the shop area, the salesman proudly handed Malcolm the pendant and inside it read, 'For my daughter, Maggie, with fondest love, your father Malcolm Baird.'

Later, as they stepped out onto the street, the early evening chill clamped down on them like a lead weight.

Sam pulled the step down from the carriage and helped Connie step up. Once she was seated, he laid a thick woollen blanket across her lap.

Suddenly Malcolm lunged forward, pinning Sam against the floor of the carriage. A woman passer-by screamed as a dark figure pushed past her and disappeared into the crowded street. All at once people were shouting and jostling to see what was going on and the assistant from the jewellery store ran out to see Malcolm lying on the street, covered in blood.

Connie was beside herself with fear for her brother and threw the woollen blanket over him as Sam and the shop assistant carried him back into the jewellery store.

Outside, the crowd had grown; some huddled together outside the store, peering through the window to see what was going on inside. Others were shouting above the drone of the crowd, swearing that they had seen the whole thing, and at least three different descriptions of the attacker emerged between them.

A passer-by, curious as to what was going on, stopped by the side of the carriage and listened to the accounts of the attack. 'Some rich bloke's been done in, by the sounds of it,' he thought.

And, as he stepped down from the kerb, his foot pushed a package under the back of the carriage. As he bent down to take a closer look, he realized that it was a gift-wrapped parcel, and the white ribbon that was neatly tied around it was splattered with blood.

Seizing his chance, he quickly crouched down and retrieved the package before swiftly disappearing into the crowd. 'Must have been a robbery gone wrong,' he told himself smugly as he vanished into the night.

Inside the store Malcolm was laid upon a *chaise longue* in the back room which they had vacated only a few minutes earlier. Connie knelt by her brother's side with tears rolling down her face. And as she studied his pale face, she was sure that he was dead.

'A doctor is on his way, Ma'am,' said Sam as he led her to a chair where a young shop assistant waited anxiously.

Jessie Kirk walked through the village on her way home from the Hall, wrapping her shawl tighter around her shoulders as the north wind made her shiver. But it wasn't just the wind that rendered her stone cold, but the memory of William Baird's hand's pawing at her earlier as she scurried from the kitchen along to the drying room at the Hall.

She had been well warned about his antics around the place when she first started to work there. But coming upon him in the most unlikely place in the house frightened the living daylights out of her.

Although no harm had come to her, the very thought of his slimy face laughing into hers was enough to turn her stomach. Unlike most of the housemaids, she didn't find him the least bit handsome. In her opinion, he was nothing but a spoiled, lazy excuse of a man.

As she passed the old shack beside the graveyard, she slowed her step as she heard someone inside scream. The next minute the wooden door was thrust open and someone ran out onto the street.

'Oh my God!' shouted Jessie as she jumped backwards and almost fell over. It took her a minute to realize that it was Maggie Brown and, as she sighed with relief, she said, 'What the hell is going on? I nearly jumped out of my skin, so I did.'

'I'm sorry,' replied Maggie as she stood on the street shivering, her hands clasped onto the sides of her skirts holding them up to her knees.

'I saw a rat the size of a cat in there and it ran over my feet,' she said as the very thought of it sent her dancing from one foot to another, shaking her skirts as she hopped around.

Suddenly Jessie started to laugh, and the shocked expression on Maggie's face made her laugh even harder.

'Well, I'm pleased to be so entertaining,' she said with a scowl on her face before marching back into the shack and picking up her bags.

'What are you doing in there in the first place?' asked Jessie.

'Oh, it's nothing,' said Maggie, hoping that she sounded convincing. 'Anyway, I think I'll go and visit my mother's grave.'

'Are you daft?' asked Jessie, astonished that anyone would want to go near that place in the dark. 'It's pitch black!' she said.

And, as Maggie turned to face her, it was then that Jessie saw the tears running down the girl's face. 'Oh my God, what has happened to you?'

Suddenly it all became too much for Maggie as she slumped to the ground and gave way to her tears. Great racking sobs shook her body as she sat there with no home, no mother and kicked out of her friend's house, accused of the most horrible crime.

Jessie went to her and took off her shawl and wrapped it around the broken-hearted girl.

'You can't sit here in this state,' said Jessie. 'Come home with me the now, till you get yourself sorted out.'

With no resistance left in her, Maggie got up and clung onto Jessie's arm as they made their way along the street. As they walked along Main Street, Jessie said, 'My da will be in, but he won't mind you being there. And, although he drinks too much, he's a good man at heart. He always liked a drop of the Johnnie Walker, but since me ma died, he's got really bad at times; but he's harmless enough.'

The Kirks' cottage sat on its own, two hundred yards out of the village itself, and had once been full of laughter.

In the early days of their marriage, John Kirk had been a hard working cabinet maker. They had had four children in all; three died in infancy and the fourth was Jessie. She had been the smallest of them all and her mother would sit over her, worrying herself sick, believing that her tiny child would surely perish. Yet she proved to be the strongest of them all.

Jessie's father had given up on life after her mother died, and his only occupation now was doing odd jobs around the villages from Beith to Barrmill, for his whisky money.

When they reached the cottage, Maggie hesitated, wondering what kind of reception she would receive. She was getting used to people in the village looking down on her and she wished she was in her own cottage away from them all.

Jessie called out, 'I'm home, Da. We have a visitor.' She turned to Maggie and said, 'Come on then, get yourself in.'

When they walked into the kitchen, John Kirk was ladling out rabbit and potato stew into two bowls. The kitchen was warm, clean and homely and, as he looked up from the range, he said, 'Oh hello, lass.'

He stopped as he regarded the bedraggled-looking Maggie standing a little behind Jessie.

'Da, this is Maggie Brown, you know, from Thistle Cottage. They threw her out of her home and I came across her in the shack by the graveyard, so I brought her home with me.'

'For God's sake, lassie, you must be starving,' he said. 'Here, sit yourself down and get some of that down you.'

He put a bowl of food onto the table for her. His heart went out to the girl as he said, 'I was real sorry to hear about your ma, lass. Now get tucked into that, there's plenty to go round.'

As Maggie sat beside Jessie, she whispered, 'I have to tell you how I came to be in the shack.'

'Well, eat your food and you can tell me later,' the girl whispered back.

Robert had been held back at the farm while one of the herd had a difficult delivery. When at last the calf was born strong and sturdy, he washed and changed as fast as he could and ran all the way to the village.

On reaching the shack, he was not surprised to find it empty, as it had gone half past seven. He crossed the street and made his way to Baxters' shop and just as he reached it, Katy's father opened the door on his way out.

'Hello, Mr. Baxter,' said Robert. 'I was wondering if I could have a word with Maggie?'

In answer to his enquiry, Hugh Baxter said, 'You better speak to that lot in there.' Then he hurried off down the street.

Confused by the man's manner, Robert was about to knock on the door when Katy appeared. 'How are you, Katy?' he asked. 'Could I see Maggie for a few minutes?'

Katy hung her head and kept her eyes looking downward. 'What's wrong? Is Maggie alright?'

Still Katy could not look at him. Robert broke out in a cold sweat as fear gripped a hold of him like a vice. He grabbed Katy by her shoulders and said, 'Katy, for God's sake, what has happened?'

Just then her mother appeared at the door.

'Bring the lad in off the street, for God's sake, or the whole place will be turned out,' she said.

As they entered the house in silence, Robert's heart was beating so fast that it felt fit to burst. He was desperate to find out what was going on, but at the same time dreading what they had to say.

Once inside the back room, Nelly said, 'You tell him, for I can't stand another minute of this day so I'm off upstairs.'

'Where is she?' implored Robert.

'Sit down and I'll tell you.'

'I can't sit down, Katy. What the hell is going on?'

Katy took a deep breath and said, 'This morning when Aggie turned up for work, she went into labour and had the bairn here. But while that was going on, me and Ma were busy helping her along when Ma asked Maggie to go upstairs and get a shawl.

'When she didn't come down for ages, Ma went to get her and she was on top of my da, fumbling with his privates and her knickers were lying beside her on the floor.'

All colour drained from Robert's face and for a split second he thought he was going to vomit, as all strength left him.

Katy said, 'I told you to sit down. Here, sit on that chair and I'll get you a drop of my da's whisky.'

Suddenly Robert shot forward and grabbed hold of Katy and spun her round to face him. 'I don't believe you, Katy Baxter!' he shouted as he shook her by the shoulders.

'You're telling me that a lass the size of Maggie managed to force herself on your da and jump on top of him?'

'Aye, that's exactly what she's telling you for I saw it with my own eyes, boy,' said Nelly who had run down the stairs when she heard the shouting.

'Where is she, Katy?' he asked, ignoring Nelly.

'I'll tell you where she is; she's on the streets where her sort belong, that's where she is,' shouted Nelly.

'Ma, for God's sake, he's in a bad enough state without you going off like a fog horn.'

'Never mind, I'll ask the man himself,' said Robert before he left the house.

'Get after him!' Nelly pushed her daughter out of the door.

As Katy caught up with him, she grabbed hold of his arm. 'Robert, please don't make trouble down at the pub.'

'Stay out of it, Katy,' he said as he brushed her off his arm.

'No, I can't stay out of it. That's me da you're after and he's no match for the likes of you in this state. Think of what it would do to me ma having you rolling into the pub asking all sorts of questions that has nothing to do with anyone else.'

'Your ma should have thought of that before she went blabbing her mouth off.'

'Robert, hear me out!' she screamed at the top of her voice as she clung onto his shoulders, forcing him to face her. 'I know how you feel about Maggie, but the truth is very different from the idea you seem to have about her.'

'What the hell does that mean?' he demanded.

'You don't know her like I do,' she said. 'She knows men, Robert. Lots of men…'

'Get to hell away from me, Katy Baxter!' he pushed her off and headed straight for the pub.

When he reached the Starr Inn and threw the door open, all chatter stopped as he entered looking like he was ready to kill someone.

'My, lad, you're in a right state the night,' said the landlord as he walked round from the bar knowing full well that Robert was out for war.

'I just want a word with Hugh Baxter,' he said as he approached Baxter sitting at the end of the bar.

'What's up with yea, man?' asked Hugh.

Bending close to his ear, Robert said, 'Come outside and I'll tell you exactly what's up with me.'

Fearing the worst, Hugh tried to calm the situation down by offering Robert a drink.

'I don't want a drink,' said Robert, the quiet tone of his voice unnerving Hugh as he stood up.

As they left the pub, a few of the locals made to follow them but were stopped by the landlord, who said, 'Go out there and you don't get back in. Now leave them to their own business.'

Once outside, Robert said, 'Your Katy tells me that Maggie Brown has a fancy for you; so much so that she tried to take what belongs to your Mrs. And I'm here to tell you how I see it.'

'Now just a minute, lad,' said Hugh.

'Shut it, or so help me I'll have you in the ground before the night's out,' said Robert. 'As I was saying, I see it like this: there she was, a young, beautiful innocent lassie living in your stinking hole and you decided to take her down.'

'Now, wait a minute here,' said Hugh, 'that lassie's a bad yin…'

But before he could utter another word, Robert set about him like an enraged animal. The first punch sent Baxter reeling backwards into the narrow path by the side of the pub.

'You dirty old bastard,' growled Robert as he dived on him again, repeatedly punching him on the face until his features were lost as they became covered in blood. And he would have continued punching him if it hadn't been for Katy and her mother pulling at him, begging him to stop.

As he left Baxter lying on the ground, he turned to Nelly and said, 'I'm sorry for the state I've left your man in, but I'm not sorry for doing it.'

Later, as Katy sat in the back room of the shop listening to her mother ranting on about how bad Maggie Brown was, she never let on that she knew Maggie was innocent. For she had found the knickers that her father had said Maggie took off herself. And they were torn to shreds.

Robert had looked everywhere that he thought Maggie might have gone, but he couldn't find her. Feeling dejected as he was leaving the graveyard, his heart almost stopped when he saw a lassie off in the distance near the shack.

'Maggie!' he called as he ran toward the shack.

'Hello, Robert,' said Jessie as she dropped her shawl down from her head.

Robert was so shocked that he couldn't answer Jessie, and his disappointment was crushing.

'Robert, Maggie asked me to come and tell you that she is staying with us for the time being.'

'Oh, Jessie, thank God!' he said as he went to her. 'Is she alright?'

'She's broken-hearted, so she is, but my da said that it's alright for you to come and see her.'

Inside the cottage John Baxter looked at the forlorn lass sitting on the couch and he felt sorry for her. Unlike most of the villagers, he knew the true nature of Maggie and her mother, and he would never forget the beautiful thing that Lizzie Brown had done for him and his wife all those years ago. He finished making the tea and handed a cup to Maggie.

'Don't fret yourself, lassie,' he said. 'If anybody can find your young man, our Jessie can. Are you sure you'll be alright, lass? Only, I was thinking about nipping out to the pub for a couple of drams before it shuts.'

She managed a watery smile and said, 'Of course I'll be alright, Mr. Kirk, and I'm sure Jessie will be back soon.'

'Right yea are, lass,' he said as he left the kitchen.

On his way out, Robert and Jessie arrived and, as they entered the kitchen, Jessie turned to her father and said, 'Don't drink too much the night, Da.'

'Don't you worry, lass, I'm only having a couple,' he assured her as he left.

And Jessie thought he looked like he'd already had a few.

As soon as she saw Robert, Maggie ran to him and they embraced.

'Thank God you're alright,' he said and then held her away from him and looked into her eyes. 'You are alright? I mean, he didn't?'

'No, thank God. Nelly came looking for me.'

'Tell me exactly what came about, Maggie,' he said.

But before she could reply, Jessie said, 'I'll away upstairs and leave you to it.'

'Thanks, lass,' Robert said and then added, 'and thanks for putting her up. It's real nice of you and your da.'

Later, when all the talking was done, they sat by the firelight until John came rolling in the door as drunk as a monkey and singing at the top of his voice.

Jessie ran downstairs and grabbed hold of her father, and between the three of them they managed to get him upstairs before he passed out.

Before leaving to make his way back to the Shields, Robert said, 'I was hoping that I could ask your da if it would be alright for me to call on Maggie? But I'll away the now and let you lassies get settled.'

'My da wouldn't mind if you called on Maggie, Robert,' replied Jessie. 'It'll be good for the old sot to have some company anyway.'

'Thanks, lass, but I'll call in tomorrow and speak to him anyway,' he said, smiling at her. 'Goodnight then.'

Once he'd gone the two girls made some hot milk and honey while they chatted. And that night, a true and unbreakable friendship was born.

≈ 7 ≈

Two weeks later Thomas Macey arrived at Baird Hall. Dressed in a respectable suit and sporting a clean shaven face, he stood at the front entrance.

When the door was answered by a maid clad in a black dress with a pure white frilly apron over the top of it, he couldn't help but feel impressed that Regina had done so well for herself.

Once inside he was escorted into the drawing room where he was told that Madam would be with him presently. This description of Regina made him smile; she had been referred to as anything but 'Madam' when she ran the streets with the rest of them.

He stood and gazed around the luxurious room, his eyes naturally drawn to the white marble fire surround where he could feel the heat of the fire from where he stood. Although the room itself was large, there was an intimacy and cosiness to it that would make any visitor feel welcome.

His eyes lifted to the yardage of red silk damask that covered the walls and upholstery. There was a huge glass mirror with sconces for dozens of wax candles that stood on the wall opposite the fire surround.

In the corner by the side of huge bay windows stood a writing table with Sheffield-plate candlesticks, and at the opposite end sat a pianoforte.

Just as he was about to take the weight off his legs and sit down, the door opened and in she swept with all the elegance of her standing. She wore a deep blue silk dress.

'Well, well, if it isn't the Lady herself,' he said by way of a greeting.

'Oh, for goodness sake, sit down and try and act with a little more decorum,' said Regina.

Annoyed by her attitude, Macey said, 'My God, it's a sad day when you forget your old arse when in the company of your old friends.'

Angry now, Regina replied in a low tone, 'I cannot afford to let my guard down for one minute in this house. Do you understand?'

'Point taken,' he said grudgingly. 'Best be getting on with the business then, shall we?' He rubbed his hands together.

Once they were seated, Regina studied her old childhood friend and realized with a shock that he had not changed. Of course he was older, but the face still took her back to those far-off days when being cold and hungry was the way of life.

'I must say,' he said, 'when you sent Jean down to fish me out, I was surprised to say the least, but happy that you trusted your old friend enough to do the job for you.'

'Well, for your information, the job has not been carried out properly,' she replied.

Sliding toward the front of his chair, he said, 'What the hell does that mean?'

'It means that I received a letter from his sister yesterday stating that he is gravely ill following a knife attack on him. And gravely ill simply won't do. Dead was the deal.'

Rising from his chair, Macey said, 'Now just a minute, I stabbed him good and proper right between the shoulder blades and dug the blade in; all six inches. So don't sit there with your haughty attitude telling me that it didn't work. Nobody would recover from that!'

'Well, he seems to be making a good liar out of you.'

'Gravely ill, you said? And what do you think that means?' he asked as he stood so close to her that she could smell his rancid breath.

'Get away from me!' she covered her nose with a white handkerchief that was trimmed with lace. But instead of moving away from her, he grabbed hold of her shoulders and pulled her from her sitting position.

'Don't even think about going back on our deal, Regina girl, for you stand to lose the bloody lot if I care to open me mouth. So think on, Lady!' he spat out the last word.

As pre-arranged with her sister, Regina pulled the cord beside the sofa which rang a bell in the kitchen. When it tinkled, the parlour maid sighed and went to leave the room when the housekeeper stopped her.

'I'll see to Madam,' the housekeeper told the surprised girl, before heading toward the drawing room.

'Bloody nosey old bitch,' muttered the maid, once she was out of earshot.

As Jean entered the drawing room, she noticed that Macey's face was like thunder and Regina looked flushed.

'Well, if it ain't the back-up,' he said resignedly. 'I bloody well knew this would happen.'

'What's happened?' asked Jean.

'Your dear sister is too slow at handing over the money for the job, that's what's happened.'

'Oh, for God's sake, man, sit down,' said Jean. 'You'll get half the money now and if he survives, you'll get the rest when you finish him off proper.'

'I don't think so, Mrs. High-and-bloody-mighty. I tell you the attack was so bad that he won't live, you wait and see if I'm right. He's probably croaked by now, and a deal's a deal. And, anyway, how the hell do you expect me to get into that house of his sister's? The bloody place is like a fortress.'

'Well, that's simple enough,' said Regina. 'You will be put up in an empty cottage outside the village and, when he comes home, you will finish the job. Meanwhile I will send word to Constance, beseeching her to send my husband home.'

'And what the bloody hell do I do with myself stuck in Scotland in the middle of bloody nowhere?'

'You can always join the gardening staff here, where I can keep an eye on you,' replied Regina. 'Take or leave it.'

'Join the gardening staff? Not bloody likely.'

'What other choice do you have? Think about it. Think very carefully,' said Regina.

Early the next morning Maggie was already up and busy in the kitchen making a breakfast of brose and oatcakes, when John Kirk entered the kitchen. He was greeted with a warm smile.

'By God, lass, you're up and started early this morning,' he said.

'It's the least I can do, Mr. Kirk. After all, you're allowing me to live here, and I want to see Jessie off to work with something warm inside her.'

John smiled as he watched her busy about setting the table. 'And I suppose the tea is freshly brewed an' all?' he enquired.

'It is indeed,' she replied, matching his smile.

John poured two cups of tea and set them on the table as he said, 'Now, young Maggie, sit down and have a cup with me.'

As she joined him at the table she couldn't help but notice the satisfied grin on his face and she wondered what he was up to.

'You're up early yourself this morning,' she said.

'Aye, I am that, and I'm off tae work an' all,' he said with a twinkle in his eyes. 'I've got a few days work fixing up the storerooms over at the Mill in North-Bar.'

'Oh, that's great,' said Maggie. 'Aye, it is that, lass. I met the overseer in the pub the other night and he told me all about it, so I start the day and if I do alright he said he might keep me on.'

Maggie was so pleased for him that she leapt up from her chair, rounded the table and hugged him.

'I'll make you up a piece to take with you,' she said excitedly.

'You'll do no such thing,' he said. 'Sit down and finish your tea. I've got things to say to you.'

Puzzled by his request, Maggie sat down again and waited for him to speak.

'First of all,' he said, 'stop calling me Mr. Kirk. Me name's John. And second, don't tell Jessie about the possibility of me being kept on at the mill. I don't want her getting disappointed if it doesn't work out. Not that I won't work hard or anything like that, it's just…

'Well, I don't have the best of reputations here about, what with my liking for my old friend Johnnie Walker, but I'll bloody well have a good try. And I don't want you tae think that you have to work your fingers to the bone in this house, lass. The place has never looked so spick and span since my dear wife was alive, and poor wee Jessie spending all the hours God sends up at that bloody Hall makes my blood boil.'

Maggie's eyes clouded over with sadness as she listened to John and she said, 'But it really is the least I can do. Who would employ me with all the gossip flying around? I can hardly walk along the street without some comment being made. Keeping the house going is what I need to do Mr.… err, I mean, John. At least I feel that I am contributing in some way.'

'I know what you're saying, lass, but all I mean is stop being a maid and start being one of the family.'

With tears in her eyes Maggie rose from the table and said, 'Well, I am going to make you up a piece to take with you, whether you like it or not.'

Later, when Maggie had the house to herself, she sat by the table in the kitchen and thought of Christmas looming ever nearer. She had three people in the whole world that she loved dearly and she was determined to make this year a Christmas to remember.

Her mind set, she searched through her clothes and chose a dress that her mother had made her for a special occasion. It was cream in colour and made of pure silk, and Maggie had dreamt of wearing it one day. But the occasion had never presented itself.

She spread it across the kitchen table and studied the slender bodice that was embroidered with gold-coloured thread and designed to sit on the shoulder. There were short ruffled sleeves delicately covered in tiny cream and gold roses and the skirt billowed out in yards of silk. It didn't take her long to decide that this was going to be Jessie's Christmas present and she set about altering the dress, using one of her friend's old ones for size.

As she worked, her mind was already ahead to her next project, which was a set of working clothes for John. And she prayed that he would be taken on at the mill full time, as he looked delighted to be in employment. The only problem was... as he had said, his love for Johnnie Walker.

She thought of Robert and her heart beat a little faster as it always did whenever he came to her mind. It was like a warm breeze that filtered through the sadness and made everything glow with happiness.

'I love you, Robert Turner,' she said aloud, 'and I am going to make you a shirt that you can use for best.'

As she happily set to work, a twinge of guilt crept into her heart as she thought of her mother.

'I don't deserve to be this happy so soon after my mammy's death. It feels wrong somehow,' she told herself. But as she worked, she felt a strange comfort surround her, as though her mother was sitting opposite her and telling her – as she often had – that as long as she was happy, then so was her mother.

≈ 8 ≈

It was Thursday, the first in the new month, and the horse fair was being held as well as the normal weekly market. The north wind cut through the village like a sword of ice, chilling to the bone, and even the hardy farmers were wrapped up against the freezing weather.

Old Farmer Kelly had rented his two fields out to accommodate the horses, as he did every November, December, February and May.

As the traders descended on the village, shouts and scuffles broke out as each one thrust against the next, determined to get their stalls situated in the best places.

Robert was already set up on the corner of the square and he sat on the end of the cart blowing on his hands in an effort to keep them warm. But inside him there was a glow that would put shame to the embers of the cosiest fire, for he was thinking of his love.

He couldn't wait to tell Maggie of the cottage he was set to buy a mile or so along the back track outside the village. He could see it now, surrounded by a low dyke, set well back off the track with two huge oak trees to its side. It was a steal at the price and, even though it needed work doing to the inside, the building was strong and sturdy.

Suddenly Katy appeared by the cart, carrying a steaming mug of tea.

'I thought you could do with a warm drink,' she said as she handed the mug up to him.

He hesitated for a few seconds as he realized that this was the first time he had seen her since the morning her father had tried to take Maggie.

'Well, go on then,' she urged. 'It's burning my hand.'

As he stretched down to take the drink, he reasoned that he had no right to hold Katy responsible for her father's actions. 'Thanks, Katy, that was real thoughtful of you. It's more than welcome on a morn like this.'

'Aye, the winter has claimed us early this year, right enough,' she said. 'In fact, I wouldn't be surprised if it didn't snow before the day's out.'

He raised his eyes skyward and said, 'Aye, Katy Baxter, I can't argue with you on that one. The clouds look as full as a cow's udder that's overdue a milking.'

Katy laughed and put her foot on the back wheel, stretching her hand out for him to help her up onto the cart. Once she was seated, she huddled close against the cold.

'Where's your da?' she asked, noticing his eyes clouding over for a second before he answered her.

'He's away to take a look at the Clydesdales for ploughing; old Billy's past his best.'

There followed an uncomfortable silence between them until Katy said, 'How is Maggie?'

Robert smiled and said, 'She's fine and doing well.'

'That's good,' she responded. 'You know, I really miss her.'

'Well, why don't you go and see her? I'm sure she would like to get your friendship going again and she has never said a bad word against you, Katy.'

'Aye, I know, but if my Ma found out she'd go off her head.'

A slight annoyance rose in him as he said, 'Well, it's better to be honest with her, and Maggie never did anything wrong, Katy.'

She looked up at him and, as usual, the love in her eyes was lost on him as he drained the mug of its hot tarry liquid.

'Thanks again for the tea,' he said as he handed her the empty mug.

'Tell Maggie I'll call round to see her the morrow,' she said, before setting off down Main Street.

Thomas Macey wound his way through the crowded streets until the bitter wind drove him to seek out the warmth of the pub. Once inside, he tried to make his way toward the roaring fire but it was too crowded.

A voice from somewhere behind him called out, 'There's a seat here if you're fast enough.' He swiftly turned to find Alex Walsh sitting at a small table by the back wall.

'Much obliged,' said Macey as he gratefully sat beside the stranger.

'You're not from around here,' said Walsh.

'That's right,' replied Macey adding, 'how long does it take to get some ale in this place?'

'The lassie's away to get mine, so it won't take two minutes to send her back for yours.'

Walsh went on, 'You're from down south, judging by your accent. You a seller?'

Macey turned, giving Walsh his full attention, before he said, 'You ask a lot of questions.'

Backing off, Walsh replied, 'Just trying to be friendly, that's all. No harm meant.'

An uncomfortable silence settled between the two men until Hugh Baxter's face appeared amongst the crowd, struggling to be served at the bar.

Relieved to have something else to focus on, Walsh called out above the noise, 'Over here.' And, turning to Macey, he said 'Shove up a bit, pal.'

As soon as Hugh was seated beside them, Walsh made reference to the rumours that were circulating around the village.

'I hear that your Nelly threw Maggie Brown out on her ear for trying to bed you.'

'Shut your face, Walsh,' said Hugh. 'My life has been nothing but sheer bloody misery since that wee bitch entered the house.'

Walsh laughed and said, 'She must be fair desperate to fancy the likes of you in the first place. I would be more than happy to see to her myself if you're not up to the job.'

Eager to change the subject, Hugh introduced himself to Macey and the three of them settled down to a day's drinking, swiftly changing from ale to whisky. It became clear to Macey that living in a small village might not be as boring as he'd first thought.

'You must be clear off your head,' said Mabel Forrester. 'I mean to say... imagine having that slut living under your roof.'

The rest of the staff at the table laughed, and Jessie could feel her face glowing redder with every passing second.

She wanted to tell them exactly what she thought of them and in her mind she was screaming the words that not one of them was fit to clean the muck from under Maggie's boots. But she had no allies here and if she dared speak her mind, she would be sent down the road and very likely without her pay.

Just then the housekeeper swept into the kitchen in her usual fashion, so full of her own importance that Jessie had to struggle hard to stop herself from laughing.

Cook, as always when in the presence of the housekeeper, scrambled to her feet and set about pouring some tea for her in her preferred china cup. As she sat at the head of the table, she silently took the tea and drank a few sips before finally speaking.

'As you are all aware, our Christmas party will be going ahead even though the Master is still very ill. His sister will be escorting him from London but, as a consequence of his condition, the trip cannot be made for a few weeks yet. This being the case, the party will be held on Christmas Eve and you are all expected to remain quiet and sober.'

She turned toward Cook with a warning glance. Her blushes were evident for all to see, for she liked a drop of the hard stuff did Cook.

Once she'd gone, the maids wasted no time in discussing the upcoming event and how different it would be this year, but Jessie was deep in thought. She had told Maggie of the attack on Malcolm Baird in London, but her reaction was such that Jessie was reluctant to mention it again.

Perhaps now that he was coming home, Maggie's heart might soften, for the Master had been good to them and Jessie was sure that he hadn't used her mammy in the way Maggie had feared.

Suddenly Jessie was startled by Cook, who gave her a cuff on the ear.

'Are you deaf as well as stupid, girl? I told you to return to your duties, and instead you just sit there looking into thin air! Now get on with it.'

Jessie jumped up from her chair and ran from the room with her ear burning and her humiliation at an all-time high, as the rest of the staff laughed at her affront.

Once she reached the drying room, her tears flowed down her cheeks and for the umpteenth time she wished she could walk out of this place with all its nastiness and never look back.

The next day Katy made her way to the Kirks' cottage, wondering what kind of reception she would receive. She knew full well that Maggie was innocent of the crime against her father, and she also knew that most of the men in the village would be only too happy to lay with her if they had half a chance.

Maggie was different somehow; she seemed to attract attention without realizing it and she grew more beautiful with each passing day.

'Blast you, Maggie Brown!' hissed Katy as she faltered in her step and tried to quiet the burning jealousy that ran through her veins like a raging river.

Large snowflakes started to dance in the air as she clung to her reserve to get back in with Maggie. She had a plan for her beautiful friend and Katy was determined not to fail.

When Maggie opened the door and saw Katy standing there with the snow falling fast around her, she ushered her in and took her cape and bonnet.

'Oh, Katy, it is so nice to see you,' she said as she hugged her childhood friend.

Somewhat taken aback, Katy returned the hug and smiled. 'It's a cold one and that's for sure,' she said as she shivered.

'Come away in beside the fire and let me hang your cape on the rail to dry.' Katy's heart sank as she watched Maggie's face light up with her smile; her large green eyes shining.

'You're looking well, Maggie,' said Katy.

But before she could say anything else, Maggie bade her to sit by the fire as she said, 'You don't know how happy I am to see you, Katy. What with everything that happened, I was afraid that you and I were destined never to see each other again.'

Katy shifted in her seat before saying, 'I thought it would be a great shame if we were to be at loggerheads with each other, Maggie… and… and I think we should put the terrible mess behind us and start again. Now, have I to make my own tea? Or are you just going to stand there staring at me till it's time for me to get back to the shop?'

They chatted for the next hour, just as they had done so many times before. But, unbeknown to Maggie, they entered a new level in their relationship, with Katy determined to make Robert her own, no matter what consequences that held for Maggie.

The next morning saw the snow lying deep on the roadways and piled up by the side of the pavements.

Ina Turner sat opposite her son in the kitchen of Shields Farm, the rising panic in her breast threatening a coughing fit. She knew only too well how her son felt about young Maggie Brown, but marriage?

'Say something, Ma,' pleaded Robert.

'Say something!' Ina replied, 'I'll say this… it's eight o'clock on a Saturday morning and I could do with a drop of your da's whisky, that's what I say!'

'Ma, hear me out… I've loved Maggie since we were bairns and I know she loves me. Are you not happy for us?'

'Happy about you and your da fighting over the lass till his days' end? Do you think I should be happy about you spending your life savings on a down-payment for a run-down cottage, away at the other side of the village?'

Stretching across the table and taking hold of his mother's hands, he asked, 'You don't believe the rumours flying around the village, do you, Ma?'

'Rumours or no, I just think it's too early for you to be talking marriage and cottages and happy ever after. There is more to marriage than sitting by the fire gazing into each other's eyes and making plans for the future. And I'll tell you why, boy. Something called life gets in the way.

'The scrimping and saving, giving and taking, learning to live together, no matter what is thrown at you. Feeding and clothing bairns that come along. Life is harsh, Robert, and survival is harsher. It's not just a question of living together, it's a lifelong commitment of putting a wife and family before yourself and working like a dog to provide for them.'

'I know that, Ma. The farm has taken years to get to where it is today and it's a constant battle with the beasts dropping, no milk, no calves, bad weather…'

Suddenly Ina stood up and walked to the range and, taking down a dry cloth from the rail, she said, 'The milk maids will be in for their breakfast, not to mention your father. Enough talk; we have to get on with life with all its drudgery.'

Shocked at his mother's outburst, Robert stayed at the table and watched her as she prepared the food. Her back was not as straight as it once had been, and the lines on her face seemed to have deepened of late. He couldn't help but think that her views on marriage were based on her own experience.

And there was his da… When he hears the news all hell would break loose and Robert didn't want his mother in the middle of another feud over his choice of bride. But his choice was fine with him and, if they didn't like it, then they would just have to put up with it.

He was going to tell Maggie about the cottage today and ask for her hand, and all he could do was pray that time would thaw the tension.

Robert said goodbye to his mother, who was sitting in the kitchen as she always did after the breakfast was over and the crockery washed and put away. He couldn't escape her pleading look that shot across the room like an arrow as he made for the door.

'Huh, away to see the vixen of the village, I suppose,' said his father. For a brief moment he thought of telling him about his plans to marry Maggie, but instead he ignored the comment and left the house.

Later, as he entered the village, all thoughts of his father were gone. He repeated his proposal over and over again in his mind as he walked.

'What if she says no?' he thought. 'What if she hates the idea of us living in Fern Cottage? What if she wants to wait?'

So deep in thought was he that when Katy appeared in front of him, he jumped in surprise.

'Katy, what are you doing out in this weather, dressed like it was a summer's day?' he asked. But, instead of an answer, Katy suddenly fainted clean away right in front of him.

'Oh my God, lass, what's wrong with you?' he said as he gathered her up in his arms and headed toward Baxters' shop.

She could hear the beat of his heart as she pressed against his chest and felt the warmth of his body. She tried hard not to shiver in the biting cold, for she had never seen a body shiver whilst it was supposed to be in a dead faint.

Once they had reached Baxters' door, Robert kicked it with his foot, his strong arms keeping Katy close against the cold. When there was no answer, he pushed against it and grabbed the handle, clicking it down. The door swung open.

Once inside, he laid Katy down on the small couch in the shop's back room. Fearful that he would leave her there whilst he went in search of her mother, she moaned quietly and opened her eyes.

'Robert!' she exclaimed. 'What are you doing here?' she asked as she hunched herself up to a sitting position.

'You're frozen stiff,' he said as he grabbed a blanket from the rail of the range and wrapped it around her shoulders.

'I... I don't know what happened,' she said. 'One minute I was sitting by the fire and the next... well, you turn up.'

'And it's a bloody good job I did,' he said. 'Where is your ma?'

'Ma?' she said. 'She's at Annie McCaw's. Oh, I feel awful,' she put her hand up to her head.

'Well, I'm not surprised,' said Robert. 'There you were out in the snow, dressed like you were going to some do with a summer dress on, and appeared right in front of me and then fainted clean away. It's a wonder you didn't freeze to death.'

Suddenly Katy started to cry. 'Don't be angry with me, Robert, I was only trying on dresses for the winter dance up at Four-Ways Farm. I never meant to get you all in a state over me. I don't even remember going out.'

'Awe, lass, don't cry,' he said as he knelt by her side and put a comforting arm around her shoulders. 'Look, I'll make you a hot drink and then go and get your ma, how does that sound?'

'No, don't do that,' she replied as she grabbed hold of his arm. 'She would kill me if she knew that I had tried this dress on.'

Feeling more puzzled by the minute, Robert said, 'Maybe you should explain, because I haven't a clue what you're up to, Katy, but I am concerned about you fainting in the street.'

She leaned back on the couch looking very forlorn and as he waited, he realized that she did look lovely in her dress; the pale blue colour seemed to bring out the blue in her eyes. He noticed too the swell of her breasts against the tight bodice and the way her jet hair curled around her shoulders.

'Well, Katy Baxter, I must say you look a picture in your dress and you'll be the belle of the ball up at that dance.'

In reply, her smile was radiant. Then she said, 'Well, I better get changed before Ma gets in or she'll slap my lug for wearing it.'

Standing up, she started to fumble with the dress and Robert felt the heat rising up his neck.

'Well, maybe you should wait till you get to your room before you start that,' he said flapping his hands in the air.

'Oh, but I'll need you to help me start the fasteners down the back. It seems to stick a bit,' she turned to look at him and he stood there rubbing the back of his neck with one hand whilst waving the other out in front of him.

'Hurry, Robert, Ma will be home any minute. It's just the top part, quickly!' she said, stamping her foot on the floor impatiently.

'Oh, for God's sake, Katy, you'll get me hung,' he said as he strode toward her whilst she squirmed and wriggled in an effort to get to the fastener.

'Hurry, undo the top part for me,' she repeated.

As he took hold of the back of the dress, he was unnerved by the softness of her skin and it occurred to him that he had never seen as much of Maggie as he was looking at now.

Once the hook came away, the whole dress fell to the floor and Katy stood there wearing nothing but her bloomers. A shocked silence fell on the room as she turned to look at him.

'Now look at what you have done,' she said. 'You must have torn it.'

Red-faced and trying to look anywhere but at Katy, Robert had a sudden feeling that they were not alone. And when he turned around, to his dismay Katy's mother was standing in the doorway.

Robert felt the blood drain from his face as he stood staring into Nelly Baxter's eyes, yet strangely they revealed no anger.

'Mrs. Baxter...' he said, trying with all his might to disguise the panic in his voice.

'Oh, don't fret yourself, lad, it's about time you two sorted yourselves out one way or another for she's been hell to live with these past few weeks,' she said pointing at her daughter, who was now standing wrapped in a blanket.

'You don't understand, this is not at all what it looks like...'

'Look, lad,' said Nelly, holding her hand up to silence Robert. 'I have walked in here and there you are with my daughter in a state of undress.

'Don't tell me it isn't what it looks like; it wasn't what it looked like when she was conceived either,' she said nodding her head toward her daughter. 'I was young once too you know, but I won't have you taking your pleasure before you're wed. So the next time you call on her, you will do so when I am here.'

She looked thoughtful for a moment before she continued, 'Though you have a lot of explaining to do where her father is concerned, after recent events.'

Turning to Katy, she said, 'I'd get upstairs and make myself decent if I were you, girl.

Anger had now replaced the shock as Robert watched Katy prepare to leave the room, seemingly without any explanation.

'Katy, for God's sake, tell your ma the way of things, you can't leave it like this...' said Robert.

But Katy was already scurrying through the door and, as he made to follow her, the front door opened and Hugh Baxter stood there looking as though he had entered the wrong house.

'What the hell is he doing here?' he asked, addressing the question to his wife.

But before she could enlighten him, Robert answered his question saying, 'Nothing is going on and nothing ever will.'

'Is that a fact?' said Nelly. 'Well, correct me if I seem to be seeing things, but you and Katy seemed to be in the throes of passion when I walked in… and thank God I came home when I did or…'

'What the hell is she talking about, boy?' said Hugh as he moved closer to where Robert stood.

'I'll tell you what she's talking about. She came home whilst I was helping Katy with the hook on the back of her dress, puts two and two together and comes up with wedding plans. But I'll tell you exactly what is going on…'

Before he could say another word, Robert felt the punch hit him on the side of his jaw and he fell backwards against the wall.

Throwing off his coat, he retaliated as he sprang at Katy's father, grabbing him by the lapels and dragging him along the hallway and into the back room.

'Now you listen to me and you listen well!' spat Robert through gritted teeth. 'I found your daughter outside in the snow, wearing nothing but a dress that she intends to wear to the winter dance. She then faints right out on the street and I brought her home, and all I did was help her with a hook so that she could get changed, when in walks your wife… and that's all there is to it.'

As Robert related the story, he couldn't help thinking how ridiculous it all sounded. And, judging by the look on Hugh Baxter's face, he too thought it sounded a bit far-fetched.

'Don't talk rubbish, boy. You came here for one thing and one thing only, and we both know what that was now, don't we?'

Unable to control his frustration any longer, Robert threw a punch that sent Katy's father crashing to the floor, hitting his head on the corner of the mantle on the way down.

For the next few seconds there was complete silence in the room as both he and Nelly Baxter stood in shock looking down on Katy's father lying on the floor, still as death.

In the confusion that followed, Robert seemed only to be aware of Katy and her mother screaming.

Jack McCaw suddenly seemed to appear from out of nowhere followed by his mother who, even though she looked to be drunk, declared Hugh Baxter to be as dead as a door nail.

Robert's whole world crashed down like a pack of cards as he found himself being led from Baxters' house by the village policeman. On the way out they passed Doctor Burnside, whose shocked expression almost brought Robert to tears.

To the right of where Hugh Baxter lay, with blood streaming from his head, lay a small box. And when Annie McCaw plucked it from the floor and opened it, she exclaimed, 'Jesus, Mary and Joseph, it's a bloody ring!'

≈ 9 ≈

The next morning Regina sat white-knuckled in her drawing room. 'Where is that stupid boy?' she said, 'I swear to God, if he has been out all night gambling, I will punish him severely.'

'And how would you go about that?' asked her sister. 'Cut his legs off, would you? He's Jack Shelly over the back, like father like son, he takes what he wants at any price.'

'Oh, shut up! You know very well what I mean. I'll stop his allowance and keep the wine cellar keys hidden.'

'Ha, that I'd like to see. You're too soft on him, always have been; even before you landed on your feet here.'

'Oh, for goodness sake, get back to your housekeeping and leave my son's business to me.'

Once Jean flounced out of the room, Regina flopped down onto the sofa with tears spurting over her eyelids and down her cheeks, destroying the smokescreen that she kept up so well. She had played her part for so many years that now she felt her past life had happened to someone else.

As she sat in the room that had become known as her private domain, fear of losing the whole lot gripped her like a vice. The thought of William turned her feelings into pure anger; he was just like his father, caring for no-one but himself.

She could see Jack now in her mind's eye, the night he left to go robbing with his accomplice.

'Don't you worry, girl,' he'd said with his usual cavalier attitude. 'I'll be back before you know it...' Luckily for her, he never did come back.

The last she had heard of him was that he had been sent down, awaiting transportation out of England and out of her life. Now everything had turned out better than she had ever imagined, and she could not allow her selfish son to spoil it all. He would be told the true nature of his background and the seriousness of his upcoming position the minute he set foot back inside the Hall.

In the great kitchen of the Hall, the staff settled down to eat their breakfast of porridge, accompanied by thick wedges of bread and butter, washed down with hot thick tea.

Mary Fields returned to the kitchen after taking the housekeeper's meal to her in her office.

'Sour-faced old witch,' she said as she closed the door and scurried over to the table.

'What's up with her now?' asked Cook.

'What's not up with her?' Mary replied, as she stuffed some bread into her mouth.

'I keep saying it, and I'll keep on saying it,' piped up Jeanie Cummings, 'something is going on in this bloody house and, if the Master dies, we'll be out on our arses, that's for sure.'

'Oh, Merry bloody Christmas to you an' all,' said Mary.

'I hate to admit it,' piped up Cook, 'but she's right, they're plotting something. I've caught her Ladyship and the housekeeper whispering in corners more than once. It's not right the way they carry on.'

'Aye, and you can bet your boots that whatever happens to us, the bloody housekeeper will be looked after,' said Mary.

'Aye well, that may be, but in the meantime keep your lugs close to the ground and if you hear anything out of the ordinary, get right in here and let me know. Forewarned is forearmed,' said Cook, nodding her head and winking shrewdly.

Mabel Forrester had waited patiently until all were seated around the table before she passed on the news that had spread around the village like wildfire. In fact, she could hardly believe that nobody else had heard! She stirred the creamy milk into her tea, all the while sending darting glances around each face as they ate.

'Well,' she began smugly, for she loved to pass on gossip especially if she was the first to impart the juicy details, 'it seems that your pal's blue-eyed boy has landed himself in it good and proper this time.'

And although her opening statement was directed at Jessie, all eyes and ears were wide in anticipation as she sat revelling in the moment.

'What's happened now?' asked Cook and, with the exception of Jessie, all the staff leaned closer in excited anticipation.

Pausing for maximum effect, Mabel eventually said, 'Robert Turner was caught yesterday taking Katy Baxter, right in the middle of the floor. Naked as the day they were born, the pair of them. When Mrs. Baxter came home, she caught them full at it.'

'Bloody hell!' cried Jeannie Cummings. 'What did she do?'

'Well, what do you bloody well think she would do? She told him to take his dirty paws off her. He told Mrs. Baxter that Katy had fainted and he was trying to help her undo the tight bodice of her dress.'

The entire staff in the room exploded into raucous laughter and Mary Field's voice screamed out, 'That's the best excuse I've ever heard.'

As the laughter continued, Jessie felt sick to her stomach and not only that but she feared for Maggie, who had been beside herself with worry the night before when Robert didn't arrive at the house as he had promised.

She had been so afraid that he and his father had fallen out, or even come to blows over her, as she was well aware of how Mr. Turner felt about her.

Jessie also knew that Maggie had sat up all night fretting about her love. She had still been in the kitchen at five o'clock this morning when Jessie got up for work.

Theirs was a love that would last for a lifetime and Jessie knew only too well how much they meant to each other. She also knew that the terrible things Mabel was saying about Robert couldn't be true. She wasn't fooled by the little Miss Innocent act that Katy Baxter loved to play.

She was well aware of how Katy felt about Robert, but would never dream of telling Maggie for fear of hurting her deeply, and perhaps harming their friendship.

Only a few weeks ago this very lot had verbally been tearing shreds off Katy for her exploits with the village lads, and here they were now giving a decent man like Robert a tongue-lashing and leaving Katy looking like an innocent bystander.

Well, she hated them all, and she hated this house with its cruel mistress and... and, oh how she wished with all her might that she could get up now and tell them all what she thought of them!

'And that's not all,' said Mabel as she continued her story. 'Hugh Baxter comes home to see Turner trying to leave the house and, when he tried to stop him, Baxter hits him over the head with an iron poker. Splits his head wide open and leaves him for dead, and if it hadn't been for Jack McCaw stopping him, he would have got clean away. Of course, they say old Baxter will never recover his faculties.'

Maggie could stand it no longer. She hurriedly stepped outside the door of the cottage and trudged across the fields, determined to get to Shields Farm as fast as her legs would carry her.

The snow was thick underfoot and in some places she found herself up to her knees in the frozen swell. Her mind was in turmoil and, while she was desperate to reach the farm, she was also afraid to learn that maybe something awful had happened to Robert.

When at last she saw the farm off in the distance, her legs seemed to move faster, ignoring the burning ache that filled them. She saw Ina standing by the window of the kitchen, and her heart almost stopped in fear as she realized that the woman was crying.

Once she reached the door, she had no time to knock for it was flung open and there in the entrance stood Robert's mother, holding her hands up to her face, sobbing so hard that she looked fit to burst.

'Oh, Mrs. Turner, what's happened? Where is he?'

'Oh lass, he's not here. They've taken him… they've taken him.'

Maggie's heart almost stopped beating as she guided the distraught woman into the kitchen. 'Here, sit down, Mrs. Turner,' she said as she tried to comfort her.

After a few minutes had passed, Ina's tears subsided and she breathed in great gulps of air as she tried to quiet the sobbing noises in her throat.

At last she spoke. 'The polis came early this morning to tell us that Robert had gotten into a terrible fight with Hugh Baxter and nearly killed him.'

Maggie sat down on the chair by the table opposite Ina, and stared at the woman as though she did not understand one single word that she had said.

Ina was quick to notice that the girl was close to collapse and her heart went out to her. 'Oh, lass, you better have something hot and sweet to drink,' she said, her own legs trembling beneath her.

'Was it over me, Mrs. Turner?' she asked.

Afraid of what the answer might be, her heart was pounding as she looked up into the eyes of this kindly soul who looked utterly devastated.

As though brought back from some haunting place, Ina realized that her resilient nature had not deserted her and knew that she would have to stay strong. Falling apart wouldn't help Robert. She shook her head as if throwing off a stray leaf that had been blown in on the wind, and looked at the girl with compassion in her eyes.

'Good God, lassie! Take those soaking wet boots off and pull your chair over to the fire. Your feet must be like blocks of ice. And, to answer your question, lass, no, it has nothing to do with you but I don't expect that fact to make you feel any better.'

'Then what on earth happened between them?' asked Maggie, as Ina knelt down in front of her and started to undo her boot laces.

Keeping her head down as she concentrated on her task, Ina explained, 'As far as we know, Robert met Katy on the street, where she fainted. He took her home and was helping her to undo the hook of her dress when her mother walked in and thought the worst.'

She glanced up at Maggie's face, but her expression was hard to read. Like herself, the girl was probably trying to work out what the undoing of the dress was all about.

'Oh, Robert, what in the name of God were you doing?' cried Maggie as she suddenly clung onto Ina's shoulders.

'Now don't go thinking the worst, lass, it'll all come out in the wash. That lassie has been after him ever since you were all bairns at school, but it's you he loves, Maggie, so don't let your imagination run rings around you or you'll go mad.'

'I have to see him,' Maggie said as she stood up barefoot and soaking wet.

'Aye and a lot of good you'd do him in your present state. You'd catch pneumonia if you put these boots back on in the state they're in,' said Ina. 'Now away into the scullery and wring out the bottom of your dress and then get sat by that fire till it dries.'

The distraught girl walked into the scullery as though she was caught up in a trance, and wrung out her skirts. When she returned, Ina sat her down by the fire and handed her a mug of hot tea.

'Now, lass,' she said, 'you have to keep a level head over this. I don't believe for one minute that Robert is interested in Katy Baxter and you've got to believe it too. There's more to this than meets the eye and the only person that can tell us exactly what is Robert himself, and he will, as soon as he gets home.'

'Home,' repeated Maggie. 'If only he were home safe with us.'

And what if Hugh Baxter died? Maggie wouldn't say the words for fear of sending Ina into a complete panic.

In her heart she knew that Robert loved her, and she loved him more than she could have ever imagined loving anyone. But had he been caught off guard with Katy? Did they have a stolen moment that neither of them could forget? And what was he thinking now? But he was not like other men… he was different; decent and true. And, like Ina said, she would have to believe that, no matter what was to come.

Later, sitting so close to the fire and with Ina quiet in her own thoughts, Maggie's eyes started to droop and soon she felt herself drifting off into the private world of sleep.

Ina covered her with a thick shawl and brushed a stray curl from her forehead. 'Oh, lass,' she whispered, 'where do we go from here?'

Sitting at a small wooden table in a holding cell in the nearby village of Beith, Robert repeated his side of the previous night's events for the third time to the two policemen sitting opposite him. Outside the cell, his father waited to hear the fate of his son.

'How much longer are they going to keep him in there?' he asked an officer who sat at a desk writing something down in a large register.

The officer looked at Tom for a few moments before leaning forward, placing his forearms on the desk.

'Well now,' he said. 'The lad's been brought in on very serious charges: attempted murder, not to mention indecency. You look like the kind of fellow that can work it out.' He smiled broadly.

After that exchange, Tom didn't ask any more questions and turned his head away from the officer, but under his breath he muttered, 'Smug bastard!'

After much coming and going of police in and out of the cell, Tom was told to go home.

'No use you sitting there,' said one officer. 'He won't be going anywhere in a hurry. In fact, if Hugh Baxter dies, your lad will be walking along the Gallowgate. As soon as the weather clears a bit, young Robert there,' he nodded his head toward the cell door, 'will be transferred to Glasgow. No use you sitting there, you'd best get yourself home.'

Shocked at the officer's words, Tom asked if he could see his son before he headed home.

In answer, the officer nodded his head again toward the door that led to the cells saying, 'Best be quick about it.'

As Tom was let into the cell, he could see Robert sitting on a wooden frame, covered with sack cloth. At the bottom of the rickety-looking structure was laid an old blanket. The gathering dusk leant an eerie sight to the small cold cell and Tom's heart went out to his son, who was sitting with his head in his hands.

As he looked up at his father, there were traces of tears in his eyes and Tom's throat constricted painfully.

Fighting back his own tears, Tom sat down on the opposite side of the make-do bed that creaked loudly under his weight. For a few moments silence hung heavy in the darkening cell, until Tom finally cleared his throat.

'Christ, lad, how did it come to this?' He did not dare to look his son in the face for fear that his eyes would expose the emotional turmoil that was surging through him.

Robert stood up and looked down upon his father. 'I have done nothing wrong, Da, except hitting Hugh Baxter. And no matter what happens now, it'll be the events that led up to that that will be the talk of the village. And, even if Baxter dies, it'll be the taking down of Katy that will be all that matters to the village gossips. I should have known better than to believe anything that sprouted from her twisted mouth,' he said bitterly.

Tom stood up and faced his son, and there came upon him a moment of sheer clarity as he looked into Robert's eyes, for he knew that he was telling the truth. The realization became so clear that he let out a low groan and he suddenly grabbed Robert and held him close.

In the moments that followed, both father and son realized a new understanding evolving between them, and a new and clear sight of each other's plight. Unashamed of their tears, both men held on tight to each other and gave way to their sorrow.

Nelly Baxter loved her daughter and came to realize that, had it not been for Katy, she would have lived a sad existence. She had grown to hate Hugh Baxter with a passion; he was a lazy spineless good-for-nothing, who thought of nothing but two things… ale and his conjugal rights.

As she looked at him sitting at the kitchen table nursing his bandaged head, her stomach tightened into the familiar knot of disgust that she knew only too well.

Aye, she had been furious when he tried to bed Maggie Brown, for she knew that no lass in her right mind would as much as look at him. She knew that Maggie had been innocent, and her jealousy had come as a surprise. But it wasn't over him that she had felt so bad, it was because of Maggie Brown.

She hated her almost as much as she hated her husband, for there was something about the girl; the quintessence of her made her allure so maddening. Not for herself did she resent the girl so much, but she knew that Katy, pretty as she was, could not hold a candle to her.

She was prepared to go along with her daughter's plan to snare Robert, because he was by far the best catch hereabouts. And why shouldn't Katy have a chance at happiness? Is it all for the Maggies of this world? Not if she had anything to do with it.

She also knew that Katy was with child, though God knows who the father might be. But that fact would have to sit on the back burner for now. Robert Turner would have to be put under pressure to marry Katy, and quickly.

The fact that he had been alone with her in the house and then the fight that ensued, not to mention the whole village putting two and two together, would be enough to be going on with.

The Turner name had been a respected one for many years and their milk and cheese business made a good living, as well as providing local employment. She couldn't see Tom Turner compromising his position in the community. After all, it wasn't as if Katy was ugly or without a decent dowry.

Though part of her wished that Robert Turner had killed Hugh, a plan was fast forming in her mind. Maybe the spineless lump could do some good for their daughter after all.

Maggie stirred and then sat up in the chair and for just a second she felt at peace with herself, enjoying the numbing effects of her slumber. But her empty-minded stupor vanished the very next second and she shot bolt upright as the knot in her stomach gripped her once more, and the painful memories bombarded her brain like a hurricane.

'It's alright, lass,' said Ina. 'You were exhausted so I just let you have some peace.'

'Have you heard anything, Mrs. Turner?'

'No, lass, I'm as much in the dark as before and, speaking of the dark, it's closing in out there,' she said as she bobbed her head toward the window. 'I've made you up a piece in mutton and the tea's just brewed, so you get that down you.' She laid a tray on Maggie's lap.

As she ate, Maggie was surprised at how hungry she was and the soft meat tasted delicious.

'Have I been asleep long?' she asked between mouthfuls of food.

'You've had a good two hours, lass,' said Ina.

'Oh my God, I should never have left you alone for so long, I am sorry,' she said.

'Don't be daft, lassie. God knows, you needed it, and you'll need all your strength to get back home, for it's getting dark out there.'

When she looked at the disappointment on Maggie's face, Ina felt sorry for her statement and said, 'Look, Maggie, it's daft you staying here hoping and praying, but you know he might not be home the night.'

'Aye, I know,' said Maggie resignedly and with tears in her eyes. 'You don't think..?'

'Not for a second,' interrupted Ina. 'Now eat up and get down into the village before it gets too dark. I don't want to be worrying about you trudging off the track and ending up in a drift.'

As she watched the girl eat her supper, Ina's heart went out to her and, in a softer tone, she said, 'He loves you, Maggie.'

Later, when Ina was satisfied that Maggie was wrapped up warm enough to keep the cold at bay for at least a while, she bade her farewell at the door of the kitchen. But before she let her go, Ina grabbed hold of the lass and cuddled her tight and, although no words were spoken, there was an understanding that passed between them and Maggie felt comforted.

By the time she had reached the road end that led out onto the main path, instead of heading toward the village, Maggie decided to turn right toward Baird Hall.

It was near time for Jessie to be making her way home and Maggie thought that her friend would welcome some company, especially as it was dark. Even if she was a miserable sight, she was sure that Jessie would be pleased not to be trudging alone, for the weather was cruel with the snow piled high.

As she made her way along the mile long tree-lined path that led to the big house, she stumbled and lost her footing, and found herself thigh deep in a snowdrift by the side of the path.

The cold shock around her middle acted like a spring and she quickly jumped out of the freezing swell, and made her way to the middle of the path whilst holding her skirts as high as her waist. When she reached the shallower snow, she shook her dress vigorously in an effort to throw off the snow from the drift. She gasped as the icy powder clung to her legs and stung her knees.

Suddenly she caught sight of movement from farther along the path, and then as she peered into the darkness she heard the sound of boots crunching on the snow.

'Is that you, Jessie?' she called as she pulled her shawl tighter around her shoulders.

The laughter that followed left her feeling colder than any snowdrift as she realized that William Baird was fast approaching and, furthermore, he looked like he'd had a few drinks.

'And what have we here?' he drooled as he came into view and stood right in front of her.

'It is I, Maggie Brown, sir. I'm on my way to escort Jessie home, it being such a terrible night.'

'Oh, a terrible night, is it? Well, that all depends on how you look at it, Brown,' he said as he moved so close to Maggie's face that she could smell the stale whisky from his breath.

He laughed softly before saying, 'I know all about you, little Miss Maggie Brown, you're the one the whole village is talking about. The little whore who tried to throw herself on an old man for a penny, my goodness!

'Did your mother not teach you to do the job properly? You should have taken a leaf out of her book. She did it to keep a roof over your head for years, with none other than the Laird himself, and not for pennies, my dear.'

Enraged, Maggie lashed out and slapped William Baird full on the face. 'Don't you dare say such vile things about my mother!'

The silence that followed unnerved her, as she stood staring up at Baird's shocked expression. He didn't move for several moments and then all hell broke loose.

'You little bitch!' he hissed. 'That is one move you will never repeat!' he spat through gritted teeth.

The next minute all Maggie was aware of was the sensation of flying through the air as he punched her face so hard that she was lifted from her feet then she crashed so hard against a tree by the side of the track that the snow covering its branches came upon her like an avalanche.

Seconds later he was digging through the snow until her body was once again visible. Grabbing hold of her throat with one hand, whilst the other tore frantically at her undergarments, he leered at her and said, 'Now I will take for free what my father paid for all of your miserable life.'

Struggling with all her might, Maggie tried desperately to wriggle free from beneath this monster that was fast ripping her undergarments off. She tried to scream but his hold around her neck tightened so much that her senses left her, and she fell limp under the weight of his body.

A crushing pain in her groin brought her out of her helpless state and, as he ravished her body, she fell into a shocked silence even though the pain was unbearable. When he had satisfied his lust and rolled off her, Maggie tried desperately not to shiver or move in any way.

If he thought she had fainted and would die of the cold, he might leave her there. After a few moments, while she heard him righting his clothes, she was not surprised when he partially covered her with snow and made a hasty retreat.

It was not until she was sure that he was well out of earshot that she gave way to her tears.

She rolled over, pulled herself up into a kneeling position and vomited violently, her body shaking so badly that the snow trapped in her hair fell in great clumps and mingled with the blood dripping from her face and the contents of her stomach.

The sky was dark but had cleared as Jessie trudged through the snow on her way home from the Hall. She was sick to her stomach at the gossip that had spun round the big house like a peerie, and she couldn't wait to get home to poor Maggie. God knows what kind of state she would be in.

Jessie looked skyward and couldn't help but stop in awe as she gazed up at the stars twinkling against the darkness, like jewels scattered over a sea of black velvet.

The snow underfoot had lost its softness as the frost had settled, making it crunch with each step like the crackling of toffee. The moon appeared from behind a single cloud and lit up the track like a beacon, casting a silver cover over the ground and along the hedgerows.

A sudden noise from somewhere up ahead startled her and she halted her step. Not daring to move, she pulled her shawl back from her ears and waited... Nothing.

Her shoulders relaxed and she sighed with relief as she resumed her trek homeward. Shivering in the icy wind, she struggled on. She looked up at the trees lining the track, their branches so heavily laden with snow she reasoned that if they were to break and fall on her, she could be lost and not found till the spring! She quickened her step and thought of the cosy fire that awaited her return.

John Kirk fought his desire to go to the inn for a couple o' drams; something in him was uneasy as he checked the pot on the range once again, only to find that the tatties in the stew had turned to pulp.

'Oh, that's bloody good,' he said aloud. 'That's all they lassies need on a night like this, they would be better off with a pot of bloody brose.'

A few minutes later the back door swung open and Jessie stumbled in, frozen and exhausted.

'Oh God, home at last!' she cried as she swiftly made for the kitchen range, opened the oven door and knelt down, savouring the blast of heat.

'By God, it's a cold yin the night and that's a fact,' said John. 'Go on now, get those wet clothes off while I spoon out your supper.'

Reluctantly, Jessie tore herself away from the range and headed upstairs to change. A few seconds later she was back in the kitchen where her father was busy pouring out two cups of strong tea.

'Da, where on earth is Maggie? I thought she was upstairs.'

John had a pretty good idea where Maggie was and his heart went out to the lass. 'After all that's happened between Robert and Katy and the rest of that bloody Baxter brood, the poor lassie's likely to be up at the Turner farm waiting to hear news of what's become of the lad.'

'But Da, it's gone nine o'clock. Surely she's not planning to stay up there the whole night.'

'She might just do that, in fact it looks like that's exactly what she's done, and who could blame her? After all, she and young Robert were planning to get wed, but after this latest turn of events God knows what will become of the lassie.'

Jessie sank down onto the chair by the side of the range.

'Oh, Da,' she said, 'you should have heard that lot up at the Hall gibbering on and on about Robert and Katy. And do you know the worst thing about it? It was the way they spoke of Maggie as if she was the worst person on God's earth. If I could get my hands on that Katy Baxter, I'd teach her a lesson she would never forget, so I would.'

'She'll get what's coming to her all in good time,' said John.

Jessie looked at her father in bewilderment. 'You think so?' she said bitterly. 'No, Da, her kind knows how to play people off one another, she knows exactly what she's doing. And whatever she sets her heart on, she makes sure she leaves no stone unturned till she gets her way.'

John Kirk watched the dawn spread over the fields as he stood at the window of his room. Last night's blizzard had left a fresh covering of deep snow, hiding all traces of the previous day's activities. It did look beautiful, untainted and pure until the village sprang to life, then everyone that trudged through it would leave their mark which could never be undone.

Funny, he thought, it's a bit like life itself. You come into this world pure as the driven snow and then life makes its mark, and whatever it throws at you moulds you into the man or woman you are destined to be. Those that want for nothing are the most selfish, it would seem. And then there were the likes of himself, Jessie and Maggie.

A sudden tightness caught in his throat as he thought of his daughter and young Maggie Brown, and where his own life had taken him. He wished with all of his heart that he could see his wife once more and feel her arms around him; his bonny lassie as he would call her.

And he could almost hear her saying, 'You're better than this, John. You can do it!'

'Aye, and I will,' he said aloud. 'I will, so help me God.'

And once again he swore off the demon drink; but this time was different. He was determined to get set on as a cabinet maker full time and get his daughter out of that contaminated midden that was Baird Hall.

Regina Baird's housekeeper had instructed the gardeners to clear the pathway of the Hall all the way down to the road end. In the kitchen the live-in staff were settling down to breakfast and were busily gossiping about the turn of events regarding Katy Baxter and Robert Turner.

'It's a bloody disgrace,' said Mabel Forrester. 'That poor Katy's been well led up the garden path by that big swine up at Shields Farm.'

'What are you gibbering about?' said Cook. 'He's only done what any other red-blooded man would do; he's bedded the two of them, but only wants to marry one. And for my money, that'll be Katy. We all know that the other trollop would drop her knickers as quick as a wink. Sure, did she not try it on Hugh Baxter?'

'Dirty wee bitch that she is,' said Mary Fields as she lowered her spoon, setting it back into her bowl of porridge. 'It's enough to turn your stomach.'

'Aye, and that bloody Jessie Kirk letting her sleep under her roof,' said Mabel. 'And, talking of her, she should have been here an hour ago. She'll be using the snow as a good excuse for putting her bloody feet up by the side of her fire, no doubt.'

'Aye, while we're all stuck here doing her share of the work,' said Mary.

'Well, rest assured,' said Cook, 'her wages will be short for her trouble and, when she does turn up, she'll not be going back down the road the night. Mrs. Mead was telling me only yesterday that the live-out staff have to be put up here so that this doesn't happen during bad weather, so she'll be sharing a bed with one of you lot.'

'Oh, that's bloody great!' cried Mabel. 'Well, she's not getting into my bed and that's for sure.'

Jessie was already exhausted from the effort of trudging through the snow on her way to the Hall. Her feet and legs were so cold that the frozen chill seemed to make every bone in her body feel like solid ice.

As she turned a bend on the winding path, she was suddenly aware of the Hall's gardeners crouching under a tree by the side of the path.

As she neared them, she saw that they were digging in the snow and by the time she was only a few yards away from them, she heard Jimmy Weir shout, 'Jesus Christ, it's a body!'

The next minute all three men lifted a frozen girl from beneath the tree.

'Oh my God, somebody has done her in!' cried Charlie Scott.

By the time Jessie reached the men, she could clearly see that the frozen body was Maggie.

'Oh God, no!' Jessie screamed as she found new strength in her legs. In a matter of seconds she was by her friend's side.

'Maggie! Oh Maggie, what has happened to you? Oh no, please don't die!' cried Jessie as she shook the frozen form by the shoulders.

'It's that lassie, Maggie Brown!' exclaimed Dougie White. 'They threw her out of her cottage when her ma died,' he said tossing his head backwards toward the Hall. 'But what the hell is she doing here?'

Frustrated by the time wasting, Jessie cried, 'Oh, what does it matter what she's doing here? We have to get her to the village and the quicker the better.'

The three men watched as Jessie quickly unravelled her shawl from around her head and shoulders and wrapped it around Maggie.

'You're too late for that,' said Jimmy. 'She's had it.'

The scream that escaped from Jessie's throat sounded like the cry of a wounded animal and two of the men jumped in surprise at the loud agonized wail.

'Shut it, the lot of you!' shouted Charlie as he bent down closer to Maggie's face. 'I've just seen one of her eyelids flicker. By God, she is alive!'

The next minute all four set about wrapping Maggie up in as many jackets as the men dared to remove, before half-carrying, half-dragging the frozen young girl toward the village.

After what seemed to Jessie like hours, they finally reached the cottage. And, just as they dragged Maggie the last few yards, John opened the door.

'What the hell?' he gasped as he took in the sight of Maggie, the Hall's gardeners and Jessie, who looked to be near collapse.

'Oh, Da, run and get Dr. Burnside as quick as you can. The men found her buried in the snow at first light, she must have been there all night!' cried Jessie.

John Kirk moved faster than he had done in years as he leapt from the doorstep and set off at a good speed, in spite of the snow underfoot.

Once they got Maggie inside the warm kitchen, Jessie shouted, 'Upstairs, the third door on the left. Bring down the mattress off the bed and the blankets.'

The men stood looking at each other for a few seconds until Charlie shouted, 'Well, you heard the lassie. Move it!'

Jimmy and Dougie sprang from the kitchen as if some unseen force had bodily lifted them from the spot, before they disappeared up the stairs.

'They don't have a bloody brain between the pair of them, standing there like a couple of lost sheep,' said Charlie contemptuously.

By the time John returned with the doctor, Jessie had Maggie laying on the mattress in front of the range fire, covered from head to toe in blankets. On sight of the doctor, Jessie gave way to her tears and leapt into the arms of her father.

≈ 10 ≈

Connie sat on a rich, royal blue sofa in the morning room of her home in Berkley Street, quietly reflecting on the horrors of the last few weeks. The Police still had no leads regarding the attack on William, and Connie had finally resigned herself to the fact that the vicious villain would probably escape justice.

Mercifully though, her brother had survived the attack, although he would be left weak from the wound in his back which had damaged his right lung. Hiring the services of a residential nurse had eased Connie's mind, knowing that her brother had the best of care.

Even so there had been moments, terrible moments, when all hope was lost for Malcolm. Now he insisted on sitting by the window during the daylight hours and became more impatient to return to Scotland. She couldn't help but smile as their conversation the previous evening came to mind; he was so determined on his return to claim his residence and his daughter.

Now she had to contend with his frustration about the Scottish weather stalling the journey home. Still, at least he was alive and she would be travelling with him. And as far as Lady Baird was concerned, Connie had a few choice words in mind for her.

Jack Shelly sat in his rented room in London's Whitechapel, his search for his old friend Thomas Macey had so far run cold. His years spent in Canada under a strict penal regime building roadways, had left him bitter. He no longer felt at ease in his homeland, for he was completely out of touch with life in England.

He had been back for three weeks and still had not come across any of the people with whom he had once shared his life. As far as Regina was concerned, he was under no illusions that she would have done alright for herself. But when it came down to it, he had been the one that had paid the price for keeping her and their son fed and clothed.

He reached under his bed and retrieved the parcel that he had covered in an old jacket, and examined it once more. The silver pendant was indeed a work of art; pity about the inscription that would lower the price of it. Still, he thought, if only he could find some of his old mates, he could shift it and get some cash.

His belly rumbled, reminding him that he needed a feed. He donned his greatcoat and stuffed the pendant into the inside pocket and headed out.

Ma Willis sat in her usual seat by the window of the Britannia pub on the corner of Dorset Street. She had already had a good few gins and, as she put her glass up to her mouth to drain the last few drops, her arm shot down hard on the table.

'Bugger me if I ain't seen a bloody ghost!' she cried as Jack Shelly walked into the pub.

'Here, Jack me lad!' she shouted above the din as she stood up and excitedly waved her arms in the air.

He looked over in her direction and a smile spread across his face as he recognized the old timer from years gone by. Her toothless grin made him laugh as he approached her. She had never been good looking, but her sunken cheeks and the lines on her face somehow tickled him.

'Jesus Christ, if it ain't Ma Willis in the flesh, as I live and breathe,' he cried as he reached her.

They clasped hands and then Jack pulled her into his arms and hugged her tight. He remembered thinking that she was naught but an old bag o' bones and she seemed to have shrunk with age.

'Well, you're a bloody sight for sore eyes and no mistake,' she said and then went on to ask him all sorts of questions about his life across the seas.

Two hours later, once they had eaten and drunk a considerable amount, Ma Willis told Jack of the whereabouts of his old friend, Thomas Macey.

'I swear to God,' she told him, 'your Regina is up in Scotland living the high life, and I would never have known, only Macey is there now getting paid for bumping off her old man. Lives in a posh house the bloody size of the whole of this street, she does, and he has money coming out of his arse he's got that much of it.'

'Is that right?' said Jack. 'And all this time I've been doing hard labour while she's been living the good life, and titled into the bargain. Well, we'll see about that, Ma Willis. Aye, we'll soon see about that.'

Doctor Burnside had ordered everyone out of the kitchen so that he could examine the young woman who was only just clinging onto life. Only then did he realize the exact nature of her injuries and wondered how this young girl had not died of shock, let alone the freezing conditions in which she was found.

He covered up her nakedness and called Jessie into the kitchen. When she appeared, white-faced and trembling, he told her that her friend had been viciously violated and that whoever did the deed had left her for dead.

Jessie fell to her knees in shock, clasping her hands over her mouth to stop herself from crying out.

'Oh, Maggie,' she whispered. 'Oh my God!'

'Come on now, lass,' said the doctor as he rose to his feet. 'You will have to stay strong for your friend, for by God she is going to need your strength in the coming weeks.'

As Jessie regained some of her composure, Doctor Burnside told her to keep Maggie warm and feed her beef tea.

'Get your father to bring the bed frame down to the kitchen and keep her out of the draught,' he said as he handed her a small, round wax box filled with a strong-smelling, dark-coloured mixture.

'Rub this onto her chest in the morning and evening, and make sure that she does not lie flat on her back. She will need to be propped up with pillows to a near-sitting position, and make sure she is kept warm at all times.'

Jessie nodded her head and thanked the doctor as he prepared to leave the kitchen.

'I'll come in sometime tomorrow to see how she is faring,' said the doctor. 'I can do no more for her, Miss Kirk, but it depends on her strength of character as to whether or not she pulls through.'

As he left the room, Jessie was overcome with determination to see Maggie through her ordeal.

In the hours that followed, she and her father set about turning the kitchen into Maggie's sick room. The bed was pushed into the recess opposite the range. A bedside cabinet was brought down and placed beside the bed, opposite which sat the easy chair from the side of the open oven door of the range.

A thick curtain was strung across the recess and an oil lamp was lit and placed onto the bedside cabinet. Lastly, the curtain was pulled halfway across the gap so that Jessie could see Maggie from any angle in the kitchen.

≈ 11 ≈

3rd of December 1988

An unexpected and unseasonable thaw had turned most of the snow into a wet slush.

It had been three days since Maggie had been found by the Hall's gardeners and, as she lay in her bed in the Kirks' kitchen, falling in and out of consciousness, Jessie had hardly left her friend's side.

As she sat and watched Maggie's still ashen face, her thoughts travelled back to the night before when she had finally told her father the true nature of the attack on Maggie. She could still see his face now as it changed colour, and then the anger rose up in him like a steaming kettle overflowing on the stove. Once he had stopped shaking, he had told her of the time when she had been only days old and her mother too ill to feed her.

Maggie's own mother had come in every day and during the night, with her own bairn tied to her breast, to wet nurse Jessie. She had given birth to Maggie three months earlier and the two bairns had shared the life-giving milk. The two women had become close friends and remained so until Jessie's mother died.

'So you see,' her father had said to her, 'you two lassies are closer than you think.'

And with unshed tears in his eyes, he vowed to find out who had taken Maggie down.

Amazed by her father's revelation, Jessie wondered why she and Maggie had not been closer when they were bairns at school. Suddenly the image of Katy Baxter appeared at the forefront of her mind and she realized that even at school, Katy had manipulated everyone around Maggie.

She shivered as she stood up and then walked to the fire and added more logs. Thaw or no, it was still freezing cold. Maggie stirred, and as quick as a flash Jessie was once again beside the bed.

'It's alright, I'm here,' soothed Jessie. 'You're safe at home with us.'

For the briefest of moments Maggie's eyes opened and Jessie held onto her hand, but when she asked about Robert, Jessie lied and told Maggie that he was on his way to see her.

Jessie was startled at the loud knock on the door and she jumped up thinking that it might be Doctor Burnside. But, as she threw the door open, she was surprised to see Mary Fields standing on the step.

'I've been told to let you know that your services at the Hall will no longer be required, so I have,' she said.

'And, what's more,' she added, 'Mrs. Mead will expect your uniform to be laundered before handing it back. Oh, and you've no pay to get because you left with not so much as a by-your-leave.'

Jessie leaned forward and looked directly into Mary's eyes before saying, 'Is that a fact? Well, you can tell Mrs. Mead to stick her job as far up her knickers as she can.'

Affronted by her outburst, Mary jumped down off the doorstep and said, 'I will tell her and no mistake, just you wait and see if I don't, Jessie Kirk.'

'Well, hurry then,' Jessie called after her as she ran down the path. 'The bloody lot of them can go to hell.'

Back in the kitchen, Jessie stood with her back against the door feeling very pleased with her outburst. She also knew only too well that once her rant reached the ears of the housekeeper and the rest of the staff, it would have grown tails.

She walked over to sit by Maggie's bed and, taking her hand, she gently brushed away a stray curl from her friend's forehead.

'Oh, Maggie, you would have been proud of me if you could have heard me telling that lot what I thought of them,' she paused and smiled. 'And I could have said a lot more an' all.'

But Jessie's jubilant mood soon came crashing down when her father came home and told her that he was not expected at his job the next day, as there was not enough work to go round.

'What are we going to do, Da?' asked Jessie as she ladled out some thick broth into a bowl and set it down in front of her father. 'What, with the Doctor's money, food and medicine for Maggie, how will we survive the winter?'

'We'll be alright, lass. I'm still bringing in a wage, only if it is for just a few hours work. Don't fret yourself, just you keep that wee lassie over there warm and fed and don't go skimping on your own food. I'll think of something.'

Tears sprang to Jessie's eyes as she watched her father eat his food. She knew that he was more concerned than he was letting on, and he was trying so hard to stay sober.

The next morning saw a watery sun rise in the sky, but there was no heat in it. Hugh Baxter sat at the kitchen table while his wife changed the bandage from around his head.

'Now, as I was saying,' said Nelly, 'you have to go along to the police station and say exactly what we talked about.'

She looked down at her husband, whose mind seemed to be somewhere else. 'Are you listening to me, you great lump?' she shouted whilst slapping him on the shoulder.

'Aye, I'm bloody listening,' said Hugh. 'I've already told you that I know exactly what to say, though I don't see what good it would do. It's the other one he's interested in and our Katy will just have to put up with it.'

'Don't be so bloody stupid, man,' cried Nelly. 'Our Katy's having this bairn. and I swear to God that she won't give birth to a bastard. No, she'll be married, and married to Robert Turner and that's an end to it.'

'Jesus Christ, woman, would you listen to yourself? The lad will most likely be well on his way to Glasgow by now. How the hell do you think it would look if I went down there and said it was nothing but a family squabble? They'd bloody haul me in an' all.'

'Don't be so daft, of course they wouldn't. Our Katy's having a bairn and I'm telling you that she'll be wed if it kills me. There's you sitting in here with a cut on your head and the whole bloody village thinks that you're at death's door.'

'Oh, for God's sake, woman, I'm going. At least I'll get some bloody peace,' said Hugh as he took down his greatcoat from the hook at the back of the door.

'There, are you bloody satisfied now?' he said.

'Aye well, just you hang on a minute, I'm coming with you,' said Nelly as she put on her hat and cape.

Hugh threw his arms up in the air in a hopeless gesture before following his wife out the door.

Shields Farm was as quiet as the grave in spite of the normal day-to-day routine. Ina sat on a winged-backed chair by the window in the front room. From here she could see the chimney smoke from the cottages down in the village.

She would not eat, and the most she had had inside her since they took Robert to the cells was some tea.

Tom walked into the room and was surprised at how cold it felt.

'Here, lass,' he said as he lifted the scuttle from beside the grate and put more coal on the fire. 'You'll catch your death sitting with the fire so low.'

As he bent down to look into her eyes, he noticed that they had a faraway, almost haunted look in them.

'Come on now, lass,' he said in an encouraging tone. 'Come away through to the kitchen where it's warmer, you'll catch your death in here.'

Ina looked up at her husband, and for the first time in years she saw love in his eyes.

'Where did we go, Tom?' she whispered. 'What happened down through the years that made us so blind to each other?'

Tom knelt down beside his wife and, his voice shaking with emotion, said, 'Aw, lass, I'm a bloody fool, for I put the progression of the farm before my family. I was hard on Robert, too hard.'

He stopped speaking for a few seconds whilst he swallowed the lump that had risen in his throat.

'I thought the harder I was with the boy, the better equipped he'd be for life; he'd be strong...' Tom stopped speaking again.

And, with unshed tears in his eyes, he went on, 'But when I saw him sitting in that cold and damp cell all alone and fighting for the truth, I asked myself how could I have hardened him for that?'

For the first time in their married life, Ina saw her husband cry, and in her breast there was a feeling rising up in her that she realized had never gone away... and that was love for this tormented soul. She held his head close to her breast and let him cry out all the regrets he'd had down through the years.

So many emotions swelled up in her, and also a new strength and determination to see her husband and son through this terrible affair that had brought them to their knees.

She clasped Tom by the hands and they both stood up.

'We'll get the best solicitor in Glasgow to fight for Robert,' she told Tom.

'And,' she went on, 'if that doesn't do, then we'll get somebody else and we won't stop till our boy's back here with us. Now come away through to the kitchen and I'll make you something to eat.'

Tom followed Ina into the kitchen, astonished by her new steadfastness, and hope returned to his heart.

Katy Baxter sat in the back room of the shop, eager to get her feet up for five minutes. The shop was always busy in the run-up to Christmas, but it seemed that every nosy bugger in the village was determined to gawp at her, seeing as how she was the talk of the place.

She looked down at the ring on her finger that Mrs. McCaw had found on the floor on the day Robert had bashed her da, and she knew full well that it had been meant for Maggie. Well, she thought, at least they hadn't missed the fact that, to them at least, she and Robert were betrothed.

Now all she had to worry about was the story her da was telling the Police, and whether they would believe him.

More snow was threatening as Hugh and Nelly Turner stepped down from the cart and tethered the horse to the rail outside the police station.

Once inside, Nelly approached the first person she saw and asked to speak to the officer in charge, who promptly told her that indeed she was already speaking to him.

'Oh, in that case,' she said, 'there are a few things that you need to know about the Robert Turner carry-on.'

'Oh, a carry-on, is it?' said the officer as he leaned forward clasping his hands in front of him on top of his desk.

'Aye well, it was all a mistake, you see,' said Nelly, digging her husband in the ribs with her elbow.

'Oh aye,' piped up Hugh, 'she's right enough. Aye, it was a mistake and that's for sure.'

The policeman's inquiring look unnerved him as he stammered on. 'Well, you see, Robert Turner and my daughter, Katy, are betrothed. And it so happened that on that night, I had had a skinful down at the Starr Inn. Well, the two young yins were in the back room of the shop when I came rolling in.

'Katy had been showing Robert her new dress and they had been cuddling. Well, I thought they were up to no good and went staggering into the room. Next thing I know, I'd tripped on the carpet and fell headlong onto the fireplace, where I bashed my head,' he paused to place a pointing finger upon his bandage.

'Just a minute,' said the policeman as he held up his hand to silence Baxter. 'Are you telling me that Mr. Turner did not actually strike you upon your head?'

'Aye, that's exactly what he's telling you,' said Nelly Baxter.

The policeman's attention left Hugh and he looked toward Nelly with an impatient expression on his face.

'You, madam, will sit over there,' he said, pointing to a seat by the wall on the opposite side of the room. 'If I need a statement from you, then I will ask for it, but in the meantime I would appreciate it if you would not comment unless questioned by myself. Do you understand?'

'Oh aye, I'll not say a word,' responded a red-faced Nelly as she quickly made her way over to the seat and sat down.

'Now, Mr. Baxter,' said the policeman, 'you were saying…'

An hour later, after repeating his story in front of another officer, the Baxters left the police station. Only once they were on the cart trundling homeward did they speak.

'Christ, woman, you're enough to drive a man to drink and bloody worse,' said Hugh. 'You're messing with justice here and I tell you, they're not bloody daft.'

'Oh, shut it!' cried Nelly. 'You've no backbone, that's your trouble. What they'll be saying now is that our story must be true. Otherwise, what father in his right mind would defend a man that tried to molest his daughter?'

'Oh, and you know exactly what they are saying about the whole daft story? Christ, woman, did you not hear the man? He has already been charged! Even if they did let him go, do you really think that he would marry Katy in exchange for his freedom?

'Anyway, you heard what the Polis said, he's well on his way to A Block in Barlinnie because they transported him this morning. Try and tell that lot your bloody story.'

≈ 12 ≈

December 16th 1888

The Hall was buzzing with Christmas preparations, and most of the staff were busy decorating the dining room for the Master's return dinner.

'I can't believe the Laird will be home tomorrow,' said Mabel Forrester.

'Aye, and his sister is coming an' all,' piped up Jeannie Cummings, 'and that means more work for us.'

'Oh, shut it, for God's sake,' said Mary Fields. 'They wouldn't be long in finding us more work anyway and that's a fact.'

'There,' said Mabel, as she sat back to admire the silver ladle that she had been polishing.

'Aye well, don't be sitting there thinking that you're the best thing that ever happened to the silverware. As soon as you've finished, come back to the kitchen for we have a mountain of preparation to do,' said Cook.

Mabel stuck out her tongue at the cook as she left the dining room. 'Bloody sour-faced old witch,' she said.

Regina Baird sat in the drawing room with Tomas Macey, who was standing looking out of the window at the snow still piled up behind the dykes and fences.

'You know, Regina girl,' he said, 'the farmers say that if the snow still lies behind the fences after a thaw, then there's more to come.'

'How interesting,' said Regina sarcastically, 'the things one learns from imbeciles is quite alarming.'

Macey walked from the window and joined Regina, who was seated on the sofa.

'By God, you play your role right to the end, eh? Well, I'll tell you this, Miss High-and-Bloody-Mighty, I've never been so happy to come to the end of a bloody job…'

'Ha!' she interrupted him and swung herself round on the sofa so that their eyes met. 'A job, is that what you call it? For pity's sake, man, if you had done the job properly in the first place then I would not have to sit here and listen to your drivel.'

'Oh, is that right? Well it won't be drivel when he cops it tomorrow night, Regina girl.'

'Keep your voice down, you idiot, unless you want every member of the staff in the house to learn about the plan.'

'Don't worry, girl, it's all in hand this time and no mistakes will be made.'

'Good,' said Regina, 'and you can stop calling me girl. You will call me Lady Baird, after all that is my title.'

Macey was nonplussed. 'Jesus Christ! You really believe that you are something special, don't you? Well I'll tell you this, GIRL,' he said with emphasis, 'Lady Baird is not the snotty-nosed, barefoot little thief that I remember, running through the streets of London pinching whatever she could to keep her belly full. So don't you give me your high and mighty act, because it doesn't impress me, girl.'

Regina was visibly shaken by Macey's words and she stood up and walked to the window, facing outward for fear that he might see the haunted look in her eyes. She took a deep breath and straightened her back before turning round to face Macey.

In a low, almost guttural voice, she said, 'Tomorrow night at 7pm, Malcolm will make his way up to his room, where he will change for dinner.'

She walked back to stand by the sofa as she spoke. 'Whilst he is in his dressing room, you will carry out the deed. I will advise him of our new butler,' she paused before saying, 'that, of course, will be you. And you will be waiting in his dressing room exactly where I showed you earlier. Do not speak unless spoken to and perform your duties exactly as I told you. Do you understand?'

'Aye, don't worry, Regina girl, I can do a bit of acting an' all.'

The look of disdain that she directed at Macey almost hit him like a physical blow.

He laughed softly as he took in the plush surroundings of the drawing room. And then he grew quiet and put his hands in the pockets of his jacket and shook his head.

Indignant, Regina snapped at him whilst spittle came rushing out of her heavily-painted mouth, 'And what do you find so amusing that you laugh whilst discussing a very serious subject, you filthy piece of scum?'

'Be careful, Regina girl,' he said, 'for any more remarks like that will get you into big trouble.'

He quickly crossed the space between them and grabbed hold of her shoulders. Shaking her violently he said, 'By God, you make me sick, woman. Just look at yourself, you're no better than the women on the street. No, at least they do an honest job for their money. But you?'

His grip on her grew tighter. 'You have spent a lifetime conning the poor bastard out of what's been in his family for years!'

He threw her from him as though she was contaminated by the plague and she fell back onto the sofa. 'Aye you're a real lady now, ain't yea? Just take a good look at yourself, Regina girl. For you are, and always will be, just a hag from the slums.'

Humiliated, but also afraid, Regina righted herself on the sofa. She had almost forgotten just how vile a temper Thomas Macey possessed. He was a hard man from a hard background and no-one realized it better than herself at that moment.

Her life of refinement had dulled her awareness of life on the streets of London; or had it? Did she so desperately crave a better life that she had all but forgotten her own? She tried desperately to regain her composure. It was on the tip of her tongue to berate him for his actions, but she thought better of it.

By the time she had gotten her breath back, Macey was pouring a large brandy from a silver and crystal decanter. He took a long swig from the glass.

'Ah, nothing but the best, eh girl?' he said before finishing his drink.

In as pleasant a voice as she could muster, Regina replied, 'Well, I think we have covered everything and so I'll bid you goodnight.'

Macey set his glass down on the silver drinks tray and, to Regina's surprise, he poured himself another.

'Goodnight'? he repeated. 'No, I don't think so, my girl,' he said before sitting down on an easy chair that stood by the window.

'I don't understand,' she replied bewildered.

'Is that a fact? Well, it's like this,' he said. 'Yea see, I don't feel easy about getting paid after the job.' He stood up and crossed the space that separated them and stood close to Regina.

'The way I see it, after the job is done, it won't take long for that nosy sister of his to find the dear departed Malcolm, and then all hell will be let loose. And the last thing on your mind would be coming round the back of the house to find me and hand me the dosh. No, I think it would make more sense for you to pay me now.'

Infuriated, Regina struggled hard to keep her anger hidden, for this man's demeanour put the fear of God into her.

'I thought we had discussed payment,' she said with a slight tremble to her voice. 'My sister will be waiting for you outside the servants' door. From there you will turn right and head straight through the field beyond and make a clean getaway.'

Macey stood staring into Regina's eyes and the coldness in them persuaded her to go along with his plan. Reluctantly she rang the housekeeper's bell, alerting her sister to come to the drawing room.

When she arrived in the room, without preamble Regina said, 'Get the package that we made up earlier today and bring it to me immediately.'

Jean Mead's look of surprise only added to the tenseness of the situation. With her heart beating fast, and not wanting to waste any more time, Regina repeated her request, only louder. Once the bemused housekeeper had scurried out of the room, Regina sat down feeling rather faint.

'Now that's more like it, me girl,' said Macey as he poured himself another drink.

Within minutes Jean had returned to the drawing room and handed over the package to her sister.

Putting down his glass, Macey crossed the room and took the package from Regina and wasted no time in checking its contents. Satisfied that the previously arranged sum of five hundred pounds was present, he made for the door.

Just before he left, he turned to Regina, winked at her and then he was gone.

Jean was in a state of shock. 'What has just happened?' she asked with a bewildered look on her face.

Regina sat down and let out a long sigh before she replied, 'He became quite violent during our discussion about the method of payment. Then he decided that it would be better if he were paid before the... event. He was most obstinate and I became afraid when he came at me and grabbed me by the shoulders and shook the living daylights out of me.

'Knowing only too well that we are not in a position to bargain with him, I had to agree to pay him tonight.'

'Well, that's the most preposterous thing I have ever heard,' said Jean.

Regina's reserve fell away from her like a lead weight and she rounded on her sister viciously.

'My God, you have a short memory,' she hissed through gritted teeth. 'You don't seem able to recall exactly where you were before I took you in and made a lady out of you, fed and clothed you, not to mention the business of setting you up here in a most respectful position.

'You just can't get it into your head that Thomas Macey could destroy everything if he wished. If he were to expose our former life in London, then I don't need to tell you where that would leave us!

'Now,' she said in a more even tone, 'go and fetch William. He needs to be told the position.'

Jean looked skyward and flapped her arms down by her sides.

'If you had given me a chance to speak,' she said, 'you would already know that he has gone out.'

'God, give me strength,' said Regina as she flounced down on the sofa and began to cry.

There was some excitement at the Kirks' cottage as Maggie had managed to get out of bed and was now sitting by the fire wrapped in a thick blanket.

Jessie was fussing round her friend for fear that she would take a bad turn, as during the past two weeks Maggie had fought a fever the likes of which Jessie had never seen. She could still see her writhing on the bed, bathed in sweat and calling out for Robert. Her chest was wheezy and the more she coughed the worse it sounded, but she was alive, thanks to God and the men that found her.

In her delirium Jessie and her father also learned the name of Maggie's attacker on that terrible night. Jessie's hatred for the whole lot of them up at the big house had become almost more than she could bear, and at times the only thing that placated her was the thought of a horrible end coming to the pampered beast that was William Baird.

She watched Maggie as she sat drinking tarry tea; her eyes looked bigger and sunken in her white face. Jessie's heart went out to her friend as she recalled the conversation that they had had the night before when Maggie had learned of Robert's incarceration in Barlinnie.

A sudden rush of icy air swept into the kitchen as John came in from outside, and closed the door tight behind him.

'By God, it's perishing out there,' he said as he rubbed his hands together to generate some heat. He took off his coat and hung it up on the nail behind the door and walked across the room to where the girls were seated.

'It's good to see you up out of that bed, lass,' he said as he gave each of the girls a peck on the cheek.

Maggie managed a smile that was sincere, for she had grown to love this man as though he were her own father.

'By, it was hard going at work the day,' John said, adding, 'I could eat a horse and that's a fact.'

Jessie laughed and said, 'Aye well, we don't have horse but we do have rabbit stew, if that's any good to you.'

'That will do fine,' replied John. 'I've always been partial to a rabbit or two.'

There was an unusual silence as they all sat round the table to eat. Maggie only managed a mouthful or two before she felt the need to lie down again.

Later, as Maggie slept, Jessie asked her da if he had heard anything of Robert. His reply was the same as that of a few days ago; the lad was in Barlinnie.

≈ 13 ≈

A light snow had fallen during the night, leaving a layer of fine powder lying over the cobbles and hedgerows. Nelly Baxter was surprised to see Katy already up and sitting at the kitchen table.

'Good God, lass, it's six o'clock in the morning! I don't think I've ever seen you up at this hour.'

'Aye well, I couldn't sleep,' snapped Katy.

Sitting in her nightclothes, her pregnancy was more noticeable now and she knew her mother was looking at her.

'Well, when are you going to start on at me for getting myself in this state?' she said as she pointed to her swollen belly.

Nelly poured herself some tea and sat down opposite her daughter.

'I didn't start on you when I first knew weeks ago, so what's the good of me going on at you now?'

Surprised, Katy sat speechless.

'You needn't look like that, girl,' said Nelly. 'Having a bairn stares you in the face well before it starts to show.' A short silence fell between them until Nelly noticed that Katy was crying.

'Oh, Ma,' she wailed, 'what am I going to do if they don't let Robert out? What the hell did Da say down at the polis station?'

'Here,' said Nelly, as she stood up and fetched a shawl from the back of a chair and laid it on Katy's shoulders.

'Now don't you go fretting yourself,' she soothed, 'things will work out, you wait and see if they don't.'

'But how, Ma? Tell me that. If they had believed me da, then surely they would have let him out by now.'

'Well, it's not just up to them down there,' said Nelly. 'I suppose it's the polis in Glasgow that have to make the final decision, but you bide your time, lass, it'll all work out in the end.'

'Aye, bide my time,' repeated Katy. 'I'll be having this bairn out of wedlock the way things are going.'

Angry now, Nelly snapped back, 'He might not marry you, Katy, have you thought of that?'

'What?' she cried back at her mother as she stood up and banged her fist on the table. 'He'll be only too pleased to wed me when he finds out that his precious little Miss Perfect down at Kirks' cottage was found passed out drunk with half her clothes missing, and her lying along the road to Baird Hall. We all know that she and her mother were sharing both the Master and the son. You tell me what respectable woman is found in such a state?'

Nelly's back stiffened at her daughter's words, for she knew in her heart that something awful had happened to Maggie and she just hoped to God that Hugh Baxter had had nothing to do with it.

'No,' continued Katy, 'I have the whole story clear in my mind about Miss Brown, and by the time I'm finished telling Robert all about her, he'll know what to do.'

She turned and walked from the kitchen and sometime later returned wearing outdoor clothes.

'Where on earth are you going?' asked Nelly, surprised to see her dressed.

'I'm going to Glasgow, Mother, to see Robert!' she announced before leaving the room.

Nelly flew along the lobby after her daughter. 'For God's sake, Katy, listen to me!' she called after her.

But her plea fell on deaf ears as Katy slammed the door shut behind her.

Two hours later she boarded the train at Beith railway station, headed for Glasgow. On the opposite side of the station stood Malcolm Baird, along with his sister and two porters who were transferring their luggage onto a nearby cart. The horse and carriage from the Hall stood on the verge on the other side of the small bridge and Malcolm's heart grew heavy as he recognized it.

Nothing would be the same now that Lizzie was gone. Connie noticed the slump to his shoulders and she was quick to reassure him by placing a comforting arm on his.

On their way over the bridge, Malcolm announced that he would prefer to go straight to the cottage to see his daughter.

'Now that we're here,' he said, 'I can't imagine waiting any longer to see Maggie.'

'Now that you're here,' responded Connie, 'it's best that we don't rush into our meeting with her. You're tired and you need to rest this evening, and tomorrow we'll go and visit Maggie. Agreed?'

'Agreed,' responded Malcolm reluctantly.

The entire staff was lined up in the reception hall to welcome the Laird back home. Connie was introduced to them by Jean Mead, who played her role as housekeeper to perfection. A private reunion with Regina awaited them in the morning room.

When they met, Regina welcomed Malcolm warmly and kissed his cheek, but the indifference in her eyes did not escape Connie's keen gaze. Once they were seated and served with morning tea and a selection of fruit cake, muffins and scones, Regina made polite conversation with her sister-in-law.

'I must apologize for William's absence,' she said, 'but his various invitations to Christmas celebrations have kept him out of late. I have reason to believe that he and Miss Elisabeth Knox have been seeing rather a lot of each other.'

She directed her attention to Connie. 'Her father is involved in many business enterprises and owns a large estate in Kilbirnie.'

'How interesting,' said Connie, adding, 'and so important that he should court the kind of young woman whose family is in a position to offer sufficient business connections, not to mention wealth.'

'Indeed,' replied Regina brusquely, for she had not missed the sarcasm in Connie's voice.

In an effort to silence her sister-in-law, Regina directed her attention to her husband. 'You look tired, my dear, perhaps you should take a nap before lunch?' she suggested.

'As a matter of fact, I was thinking of inviting you ladies to join me in a walk around the gardens,' he said, knowing that Regina hated walking.

'Oh, don't you think it's a bit cold for you to be out walking, my dear?' she enquired.

'On the contrary,' said Malcolm, 'I think it would do me the world of good.'

'Very well, dear, but I hope you will excuse me from your excursion, I feel a slight headache coming on and I fear that if I don't lie down then it will develop into a very tiresome episode,' Regina lied.

'Of course, my dear,' replied Malcolm.

Later as they walked in the garden, Connie said, 'It may be my nasty mind, but don't you think it rather strange that Regina did not even mention the attack on you in London?'

'For one as selfish as she, then no,' replied Malcolm. 'It did not surprise me in the slightest. But there is something bothering me and I can't quite put my finger on it... an atmosphere that hangs heavy around every corner like a thief in the night.'

'Yes, I sensed that something was amiss,' said Connie, 'but I'm sure that it is because you have been away for so long. Things are bound to feel out of sorts.'

She slipped her arm through his and added, 'Someone tried to murder you, Malcolm. Lizzie died and you have a great deal to talk over with Maggie. Of course things will feel odd.'

Malcolm stopped walking, looked down at his sister and said, 'You know, Connie, a great wave of anger swept over me when I saw Regina today. There she was, the lady of the house with every desire at her fingertips, and my real wife – for that's how I thought of Lizzie – is lying in her grave.

'I wanted to toss her out onto the street there and then, because it was Lizzie who should have been standing there. Oh, she would have run into my arms and I would have held her like I'd never let go, for that's how we were together.'

He looked off into the distance, and for the briefest of moments Connie saw love in his eyes.

'But,' he said, as he came back to the present, 'I have decided to leave the Hall and move into Hill View House no later than tomorrow, for I can no longer abide this place.'

Connie looked up into his face and knew that he was determined to carry out his plan. He had long wished that Lizzie would have moved into his other home with Maggie, but she would never have consented to being a kept woman. Now Connie hoped that her brother would find some comfort in his decision.

'Come along,' she said. 'Let's get you inside, it's getting cold out here.'

As they turned to retrace their steps, Thomas Macey slipped behind the high hedge to their right and darted out of sight.

It was late afternoon when Katy finally managed to obtain permission to see Robert. She shivered as she sat in the cold waiting area while the guard went off to fetch Robert from his cell. Beyond the room she could hear the clinking of chains that held bunches of keys and the eerie sound they made when turning a lock.

She looked around the cold room that was, she supposed, not unlike the cell that he would be locked in. The thick door had a wooden slot to its upper half that was pulled halfway across iron bars.

When at last she heard footsteps from along the corridor, she stood up and waited nervously, fidgeting with the ribbon of her bonnet. All at once the door was pushed open, and suddenly he was there in front of her.

The guard told Robert that he had five minutes with his visitor and then he left the room, closed the door, locked it and slid the wooden slot all the way open and stood looking into the cell.

She held her breath as she looked into his face. He had lost weight and his eyes seemed to be deeper set into their sockets, his face grey.

'Oh Robert,' she said as she clasped her hands together in front of her breast.

He didn't speak; he just stood there looking at her, his eyes empty.

'We don't have a lot of time, so I will just tell you what I came to say,' she said. 'My father has spoken to the polis, telling them that the whole thing was a mistake. He has instructed a lawyer to do the same in writing so that they will let you go.'

She took a step closer to him as she went on, 'I am so sorry that the whole thing ended up this way, Robert, and I hope that you will come to realize that it is I who is fighting for you. Maggie asked me to tell you that she is sorry but there will be no future for you and her.'

She dropped her eyes groundward, for she couldn't bear to see the hurt in his eyes over Maggie.

When he spoke, his heart was breaking and his voice could not disguise the fact.

'Katy, please, for once be honest with me,' he pleaded as he moved closer to her.

He spread his arms open wide as he said, 'I'm here in this hell-hole and I don't know what's in front of me, so please don't lie to me now.'

'I am being honest with you, Robert, and I hate to see you in this place and to be so broken, but please listen to me,' she said as she moved closer to him. 'I had to come here today for I can't stand the way she has deceived you.'

'Don't, Katy,' said Robert as he held his hand out as if to silence her. 'Don't lie to me.'

Her eyes filled with tears and she closed the gap that was between them.

'You don't understand. You see, Maggie has been seeing William Baird for the past year and I know it is hard to take, but hear me out. On the third of September, I was walking along Wyllie's track when I heard a carriage off in the distance. I stood by the side of the track for it to pass and when it got closer, I realized that it was Maggie and William Baird.

'When they stopped I saw another man in the carriage, they seemed to have been drinking and asked if they could drop me off in the village. When I said no, they grew angry and insisted that I join them in the carriage. I was afraid but I thought that I would be safe enough with Maggie being there.

As I stepped up to get into the carriage, the man grabbed hold of me and, and... he attacked me.'

There followed a shocked silence, then Robert spoke, 'Katy, how can this be true? Do you hear what you are saying? How many more lies can one person tell?'

Tears cascaded down Katy's cheeks.

'Oh, Robert,' she cried, 'I only wish to God that it was lies. That man disgraced me and now I am left carrying his child. Don't you see, if you would only give me your name so that I would not be shamed and an outcast through no fault of my own, I know that in time you could come to love me as much as I love you.

'You must wake up to the fact that Maggie is not the girl you thought she was. She was only using you when all the time she was with Baird. Robert, she laughed as that man violated me.'

She sobbed as she clutched onto him, 'You got it so wrong, Robert. Why in the name of God do you think she hasn't been to see you? What does that tell you? That it is I who has always loved you.'

'Stop it, Katy, stop it now!' he cried whilst shaking her by the shoulders.

'Time's up,' called the guard as he put the key in the lock and turned it.

Desperate now, Katy cried, 'Robert, you have to believe me for who in the name of God would tell you such a thing if it weren't true?'

Shocked and dazed by her words, Robert was led along the corridor back to block A.

'If you don't believe her, lad, then you're a fool,' said the guard who had witnessed every word. 'I would marry her myself; the poor wee lassie is in a terrible state.'

Pleased with her performance, Katy left the prison and boarded a cab bound for the railway station. As the cab trundled through the streets of Glasgow, Katy Baxter felt triumphant.

Back in his cell, Katy's words ran through Robert's mind like a steam train. He paced the tiny space from his bed to the door, intermittently running his hands through his hair.

His father had twice been to see him and not once did he mention Maggie. And his mother had not sent word of her either, surely to God there couldn't be any truth in what Katy had told him. But why hadn't Maggie been to see him?

If she truly loved him, then why hadn't she come to him or at least sent a message through to him? His mind took him back two years previously when rumours had been flying yet again round the village about Maggie and her mother.

He had been walking around outside their cottage trying to find the courage to visit Mrs. Brown to ask if he could call on Maggie. And there was Maggie at the door embracing Baird like he was something special in her life. He remembered watching her that night just as dusk was falling, but had it been Baird himself or William that left the cottage that night?

The question that at the time had been mere curiosity now seemed to hold his future in its hands. Could it have been William Baird, he asked himself over and over again until he felt that his head would explode. Could Maggie have played him for a fool? How could she and her mother afford to live in comfort?

His heart was breaking at the thought that she could give herself to another and at the same time make him believe that she loved him.

Maggie had been Katy's friend, and the very thought that she and William Baird had witnessed the crime against Katy that left her with child, sickened him. He knew that Katy could tell a tall tale, but even she could not come up with something as terrible as that. Surely to God no young woman would say such an appalling thing if there was no truth in it.

He paced the cell like a crazed animal; an unspeakable anger rising up in him the likes of which he had never known. Torn between his love for Maggie and the terrible events that Katy had recounted, made him lose all control of his feelings.

The cry from deep within him found no escape from his mouth as he gritted his teeth and in utter despair he punched the walls of his cell until his knuckles bled.

Jessie waited until Maggie was asleep before she left the cottage. She had taken sixpence out of the pot that stood beside her mother's carriage clock on the mantelpiece.

She felt heavy-hearted as she made her way to Dr. Burnside's house in the village to pay for the latest round of medication for Maggie. With her father not getting taken on full time at work, and with Christmas just a week away and very little money left, she didn't know how they could afford to feed themselves.

As she passed the old barn, Annie McCaw crossed the road to speak to her.

'I hear Maggie Brown's in a bit of a state? How is she?' she asked as she stopped and stood close to Jessie.

'Who wants to know?' asked Jessie, suspicious that perhaps Katy Baxter was fishing around to find out what had happened to Maggie.

'Well, excuse me for being neighbourly,' snapped Annie. 'For your information, I was just concerned for the lass.'

'Aye and when were you ever interested in Maggie's welfare?' Jessie snapped back,

'Well, with the news of Robert and Katy's wedding plans, I thought she would be in a bit of a state over it.'

Jessie was so taken aback at Annie's words that she almost fell over as she whispered, 'Wedding plans?'

'Aye, that's what I said. Surely you've heard?'

Still in shock Jessie replied, 'As a matter of fact, I have heard no such thing and furthermore I don't believe you have either.'

Annie folded her arms and nodded her head toward Jessie as she said, 'You want to watch that mouth of yours, for it just might land you in trouble. All I'm doing is repeating what I've just been told by Nelly Baxter herself, so don't you go mouthing off to me, lady.'

Jessie was lost for words and for the briefest of moments she wanted to beg this woman to tell her the truth, but she was too afraid that Annie already had.

≈ 14 ≈

Thomas Macey stood at the bar in the Starr Inn along with his new-found friend Alex Walsh. The village was busy in the run-up to Christmas and the inn was filling up faster than a pail under a running tap.

Knowing that he only had an hour before he had to leave, Macey ordered another drink.

'You're downing them swift the night,' said Walsh.

'I am that, me lad,' answered Macey, adding, 'I've a bit o' business to tend to shortly and I don't mind telling yea, I'd rather give it a miss.'

He smiled at the thought of Regina's face if he didn't turn up at the Hall to bump off her old man. Bloody serve her right, he thought. His smile deepened as he imagined how consumed with rage she would be, and with no way to vent it.

She would have to sit through her meal playing the lady of the house, smiling and talking, pretending that all was well whilst her plans fell apart in front of her.

The more he thought about it, the more appealing the idea became. After all, she had treated him like a piece of dirt and her no better than he was.

He laughed out loud as Walsh peered at him with such a look of confusion on his face that it made him laugh even harder.

'What the bloody hell's so funny?' asked Walsh, puzzled at Macey's behaviour.

'You wouldn't believe me if I told you.'

Just then the two were joined by Hugh Baxter, who had just entered the inn.

'What's the bloody joke?' he asked.

'Well,' said Macey, 'we were just talking about the day your wife bashed you on the head and blamed it on that poor bloke from the farm.'

'Aye, very bloody funny,' said Hugh. 'I tell you, it's a bloody wonder I'm not six feet under with all the carry-on with our Katy and that Robert Turner.'

'Pay no heed to him,' said Walsh. 'What he meant to say was that hen-pecked men stand out like a sore head with a bandage round it.'

The laughter that followed caught the attention of the newcomer that had just entered the inn. As he made his way to the bar, he glanced over in the direction of the three men standing there still laughing. He stopped dead in his tracks as he heard a familiar voice.

Surely it couldn't be Thomas Macey? He stared in disbelief.

'By Christ, it is!' he said aloud as he made his way over to the three men sitting at the far end of the bar.

Just as he walked toward the men, Macey turned around and came face to face with his old friend, Jack Shelly.

The two men stared at each other for a few seconds before Shelly said, 'Jesus Christ, man, I never thought I'd see you! Not in a bloody million years.'

Macey rose from his stool and, before any more words were spoken, the two men embraced each other warmly.

'Bloody hell, man, I never thought I would come across you in a small village in Scotland,' said Shelly.

Thomas Macey's eyes were wide with the shock of seeing his old friend and it seemed like minutes passed whilst they stood just looking at each other.

'Jack Shelly, I'll be damned!' Macey managed at last. 'When the hell did you get back?'

The two men moved away from the bar and found a seat by the fireplace where they talked without stopping for the next hour.

Regina Baird almost fainted with fright when she saw Malcolm escort his sister, Constance, into the dining room.

Noting the horror on her face, Malcolm asked, 'Are you feeling ill, my dear? You look as though you have taken quite unwell.'

Unable to answer him, Regina gasped as though she had just surfaced from deep water, whilst she pulled at the collar of her dress. Her face grew pale and her eyes enlarged to such an extent that they appeared to bulge from their sockets.

Two maids rushed to her side as her legs gave way, threatening to send her dropping to the floor.

'Send for the doctor at once,' ordered Malcolm, as two more staff appeared and helped get Regina into the morning room and onto a sofa.

'Please leave me,' said Regina as the maids ran from the room.

'I do not need a doctor,' she snapped at Malcolm and Connie, who were standing next to the sofa.

'But you obviously took some kind of a fit and then almost fainted,' declared Connie.

Regaining her senses, Regina repeated, 'I do not need a doctor, and I would be grateful if you would kindly respect my wishes.'

'Very well, my dear,' said Malcolm, 'I will see to it that the doctor is not summoned, but in the meantime I do think you should be escorted to your bed. You are still very pale.'

The housekeeper was made aware of the events surrounding Lady Baird as she made her way from the servants' quarters. What the hell has happened, she thought, as she made her way to Regina's room. And where on earth was Macey? He should be making his way over the back field by now, having finished off Malcolm.

When Jean entered her sister's bedroom, it was to see her pacing around the room like a caged animal.

'For God's sake, I thought you were on your deathbed by the way the staff was acting,' said Jean.

'I might as well be on my deathbed, for Malcolm is not. He's alive! He's alive!' shouted Regina.

'For God's sake, woman, keep your voice down or the whole house will hear you!' hissed Jean through gritted teeth. 'I know full well that he is alive, for Macey did not appear by the back door as we had planned.'

In tears, Regina turned to her sister. 'What are we going to do?' she sobbed. 'I should never have paid him before the job was done. I should have known better than to trust the likes of him. For all we know, he could be well on his way back to London by now with my money.'

She stopped wailing suddenly as a thought struck her. 'William,' she said. 'Where is he?'

'William?' repeated Jean. 'He must have sloped off this morning. The only reason I know that he has been home is the fact that his bed had been slept in.'

Regina walked across the room to her window and pulled on the heavily embroidered curtains. As she looked out into the dark night, a plan was forming in her mind. She turned around to face her sister, who was watching her intently.

'I'll do it myself, by God I will,' she said.

'Aye, and how do you think that is going to happen?' asked Jean.

'Oh, use your brain,' snapped Regina. 'Rat poison! And you as housekeeper know where it is kept, and you will bring it to me without any further delay.'

'Have you gone mad? Just listen to yourself, woman,' said Jean. 'You can't do this in a panic; we have to plan it.'

'We have no time to plan it. Don't you see that it is your future that is at stake as well as mine? And William, where is he when I need him most? The selfish swine cares for nothing but his whores and his gambling.'

She started to pace the room again, twisting her hands in anguish.

As Jean watched, she realized that if nothing was done then Regina herself would bring everything crashing down.

'Listen to me,' said Jean, as she took hold of her sister by the shoulders and backed her onto a chair near the window. 'I will put the rat poison in his after-dinner drink, if you promise not to get involved.'

Regina stared up at her sister, her eyes filling with tears. 'Very well, I will leave it in your hands,' she agreed. 'But I warn you,' she added, 'you must be aware of Constance at all times.'

'Of course,' said Jean, 'now I will make up a tray for you, and send Mary in to get you undressed and into bed.'

Once she had left the room, Regina once again stood looking out onto the gardens below. A light snow was falling gently to the ground and the beautiful sight only irked her. This place in its entire splendour was hers and she would fight till the end to keep it.

Downstairs in the kitchen Cook had spent most of the evening sipping on a bottle of wine that she had taken from the cellar. The rest of the staff were busy running backwards and forwards to the dining room where Malcolm and Connie were enjoying their meal.

Before Jean could order a tray for Regina, Mary Fields had come back into the kitchen and informed them that the Mistress was feeling much better, and she was to take up some tea before helping her get dressed.

'Bloody woman,' thought Jean, 'what the hell is she doing now?'

She returned to her office and sat by the fire, pondering how she would get the poison into Malcolm's drink and how to ensure he would receive it, as she was not in the habit of serving drinks in the sitting room. For his wife to serve them drinks was just not done. However the night turned out, Regina would be at the centre of events and that's for sure, thought Jean.

In the sitting room Malcolm said, 'Damn that woman! I wanted to discuss our forthcoming separation tonight.'

He fell silent for a few moments, before saying, 'It can't have been easy for her all these years. I suppose she realized that she didn't really love me from the moment she set foot in this house. I can't help but feel sorry for her because hers has been a lonely existence here.

'If she had been willing, I would have suggested setting her up in a house in London and giving her a substantial monthly allowance, but she seemed to become part of this place. No, it would be very wrong of me to suggest that she live anywhere else. And, as for William, he is his own man and unfortunately his upbringing in this house has turned him into the person that he is, selfish and lazy.'

Connie looked into her brother's eyes and said, 'Don't reproach yourself, Malcolm, just remember how selfish Regina has been from the very start. It was she who drove most of your friends away, not to mention getting rid of all of the staff.

'She shut you out of William's life and turned him into the pompous creature that he is today. She banned you from her bed and decided to stop all the balls and parties that once lit up Baird Hall. Don't feel sorry, Malcolm, for she has lived to her rules throughout your entire marriage.'

An hour later Regina joined her husband and his sister in the sitting room. Malcolm rose to his feet when his wife entered the room.

Extending his hand to her, he said, 'You look much better, my dear.'

Connie added, 'I'm glad you feel better, Regina. I fear the journey has tired me out and I must retire. I do hope you will excuse me?'

'Of course,' answered her sister-in-law, adding, 'I trust you will have a comfortable night.'

Once she left the room, Regina felt more relaxed. She was more than happy to see her sister-in-law leave.

A few seconds passed in silence as Malcolm struggled to find the right words that would leave his wife in no doubt that their marriage was over, and had been for many years. Looking at her, he saw no trace of the young woman that he had once loved, even if it had only been for a short time. From the moment she entered the Hall she had changed, and her influence upon his home had gradually removed all its character until it became his prison.

'Regina…' he started. 'For many years now, you and I have been apart, although living in the same house. I know you value your standing in the community and a scandal would make you feel most uncomfortable. But what I am saying to you is that we can no longer live under the same roof, for we are in all fairness nothing more than strangers.

'It is not my intention to seek a divorce, however I have decided to quietly move into Hill View House. I will, of course, be seen to visit the Hall and will also arrange for you to receive a substantial monthly allowance. However, there is an alternative solution you may also wish to think about, which would remove you from the scandal which will surely occur once we separate. Of course, I would provide a considerable residence for you.'

Regina was confused. 'What do you mean, scandal?' she asked.

'I will be laying claim to my daughter... Maggie Brown,' he answered.

Regina stared at her husband in disbelief. 'Is this some kind of a nasty prank, Malcolm? Because I do not find it in the slightest way amusing!'

'Nasty prank?' he repeated angrily. He rose from his chair and crossed the space between them to stand in front of her.

Bending from the waist so that he was at eye level with her, he spat out his words, 'How dare you! How dare you!' he repeated. 'You have the audacity to sit there and call my beautiful daughter a nasty prank!'

Regina stood up, her breast heaving with indignity, her eyes blazing and so full of hatred that they appeared to deepen in colour.

'How dare I?' she hissed. 'You are telling me that you have a bastard from an adulterous union and you expect me to understand, is that it? Run away back to London where I would be spared the gossip? Oh no, no, I will not leave my home under any circumstances. Do I make myself clear?'

Malcolm was incensed by her words. 'Oh yes, you make yourself perfectly clear!' he shouted.

'The Lady of the Manor will have her home and everything of value in it, for that's all you ever cared about, Regina. Don't take me for a complete fool, for I knew from the very moment you stepped foot in this house that you were determined to see this day. Oh, it took twenty years, and I congratulate you on your enduring persistence, but you are welcome to this house.

'Do you know what you have turned it into?' he roared at her. 'A cold and empty shell that has been stripped of all its character, its warmth and its beauty.'

Regina rounded on him, her anger matching his as she spat out her words, 'Don't think your bastard child will take my son's inheritance away from him, for he is legally entitled as your adopted son.'

Malcolm suddenly laughed and shook his head in a contemptuous manner as he stared at this woman, whom a meaningless certificate of marriage deemed to be his wife.

'Let me tell you this...' he said in a strong and even voice, 'my daughter's mother was the most wonderful human being in existence and, had I been a better man, I would have seen to it that you and your son were divorced from me and my ancestral home years ago.'

The raised voices had created quite a stir in the house and had attracted Mabel Forrester and Mary Fields, whose ears were pressed hard against the sitting room door.

'Bloody hell!' whispered Mary. 'Them two won't stop till one of them is dead and that's a fact.'

'Quick, let's get out of here before somebody finds us with our lugs stuck to the door.'

The two girls ran to the kitchen and burst through the door like the devil himself was after them.

'Jesus Christ! You scared the bloody life out of me, bursting in here like that,' said Cook, who was more than a little tipsy.

'Oh, you'll never guess, not in a bloody million years,' cried Mary, adding, 'the Master is Maggie Brown's father and he wants a divorce and she won't leave because of her William and...'

'Oh, for Christ's sake,' shouted the cook, 'slow down and give us the full story.'

Mary took a deep breath and was preparing herself to tell all whilst Mabel took a swig out of Cook's bottle. Suddenly they were silenced by a scream, followed by a scuffle coming from the corridor.

When the kitchen door burst open, they were amazed to see two men pushing the housekeeper into the kitchen.

'Stay right there, Jean, me girl,' said the man known as Mr. Macey, who had visited the Mistress earlier in the week.

The housekeeper's face was scarlet as she was callously thrown against the large wooden table, scattering the kitchen maids who had been sitting there.

'Bloody Hell!' cried Jeanie Cummings as she ran across the kitchen. 'What the hell's going on?'

'It's none of your business,' answered the housekeeper, 'so you can just get back to work.'

'Not bloody likely,' cried Jeanie as she clasped her hands excitedly. 'We've got a right to know what's happening; after all, we live here.'

'I don't mind you girls hearing what I have to say to your mistress,' said Jack Shelly, who was determined to wreak revenge on his wife after hearing the full story of her life of luxury earlier in the inn from Thomas Macey. He looked at Macey, who was standing by his side at the kitchen door.

Jack Shelly directed his attention toward Jeanie Cummings.

'Would you be kind enough to show me where I can find your mistress?' he asked.

'Aye,' answered the maid with a smile on her face, 'just follow me this way.' She hurried along the hallway.

'Who shall I say is calling?' asked Jeanie, directing her question to Shelly.

'Oh, no need to introduce me, girl,' he said. 'She knows me alright.'

When they reached the sitting room, Jeanie knocked on the door and the raised voices within the room fell silent.

The Curse of Baird Hall

When the maid opened the door, Jack Shelly walked straight into the room and stared at the woman that he had last seen twenty years earlier when he left her in their basement dwelling in Whitechapel.

She was standing by a large leather chair, her dress of maroon velvet looked exquisite, and her hair was pulled back and styled in soft ringlets that lay against the sides of her neck.

'What do you men think you are doing barging into my home in this fashion?' asked an astonished Malcolm.

'Well, you see, Sir,' said Shelly, as he walked farther into the room. 'I could ask you what you are doing here with my wife?'

Regina screamed and fell backward onto the chair, holding her hand up to her forehead. The colour had drained from her face and a nervous tick took hold of her left eye, making it look like she was blinking rapidly.

'What are you talking about, man?' demanded Malcolm.

'I'll tell you what I'm talking about, Squire, this here is my wife, Regina Shelly, who lived with me and our son, William, in Whitechapel. I left her to go thieving, which was our only source of getting money for food.

'Me and my accomplice walked straight into a trap and the Peelers caught us red-handed. Well, I ended up getting shipped abroad to do my time and when I gets back, the bold Regina here has up and married a gentleman.'

He stuffed his hand inside his jacket pocket and took out a crumpled piece of paper and handed it to Malcolm. 'Here you are, Squire, read it for yourself.'

Malcolm read the contents of the paper that stated that a marriage between Regina and Jack Shelly had taken place in London on the tenth day of January 1865.

Malcolm sat down by the small round table that stood by the side of the window and laid the marriage certificate on its polished surface. He looked at Regina, who sat on her chair with a handkerchief pressed to her mouth, her eyes bulging.

A terrible anger swept through him like a high tide, as he recalled the heated argument he and Regina had before, and all she wanted was his home, his name and his fortune.

He clenched his fists and his body began to shake as he remembered his frustration throughout the years when he had thought he was not free to marry Lizzie. Lizzie, who was the love of his life and had wanted nothing from him but his love; Lizzie, who lay in her grave as this lying piece of filth led the life that should have been hers. How could he have been so stupid? His Maggie living in a cottage whilst William Shelly enjoyed a pampered lifestyle thanks to his mother, who was nothing more than an imposter.

In the confusion that followed, Malcolm was aware that Connie was by his side as Regina, with no trace of refinement in her voice, screamed obscenities at Jack Shelly. It seemed that the whole of the Hall's staff were outside the room and when Shelly saw Jean Mead, he pointed her out.

'Oh, and this one here, Squire, is none other than her conniving sister. So there you go, you've been had good and proper.'

Malcolm walked across the room to where Regina sat shocked and as still as a statue. Bending toward her, he suddenly grabbed her forearms with both hands and dragged her from her seat. As he marched her along the hallway, past the goggle-eyed staff, he looked as though he was about to kill her.

Her protests fell on deaf ears as he threw open the main door of the house and thrust her out into the night. He then turned around and ordered Mead from his house. Finally, when he returned expecting to find the two men waiting there, he was surprised to find them gone.

Connie quickly took the situation into her hands and ordered the staff back to their quarters, asking Mary Fields for a tray with brandy and a pot of hot water to be brought to them immediately.

In the kitchen the staff were buzzing over the night's events.

'Imagine her lying to him all these years,' said Mabel. 'And,' she added, 'Maggie Brown is really Maggie Baird and that bloody stuck-up cow that called herself the Housekeeper is really the Mistress's sister and no bloody better than the likes of us. Oh, it's all too much for a body to deal with.'

≈ 15 ≈

The next morning in the kitchen of Shields Farm, Ina Turner was incensed when Tom finally told her of the attack on Maggie. He was telling her now because one of the dairy maids let it slip earlier that Maggie, by all accounts, was on her death bed.

Raging at him, Ina screamed at the top of her voice, 'I don't understand you, Tom Turner! That lass is the love of your son's life and you don't even bother to tell me that she is at death's door. What the hell is the matter with you, man?'

She raged on, 'Robert is sitting in a prison cell in Glasgow, wondering why the hell Maggie has not so much as set foot out of the village to go and see him. And all the time you knew what had happened to the lass. You make me sick, Tom Turner, you make me sick.'

She sat down at the table and cried. Tom poured his wife a mug of hot tea before he sat opposite her.

'Ina,' he began. 'When they took our Robert away, I was deathly afraid that you would end up ill with the worry of it all. As it was, you nearly went out of your mind over the whole bloody mess. Do you really think that I was hard enough not to tell you because I didn't care? For Christ's sake, Ina, don't you think you had enough on your plate?

'I am the man that sits alone in my bed while you scuttle about down here sobbing your heart out. Oh aye, that would just have been the right thing to tell you when you were already half-mad at the plight of our son. Come on now, lass,' he said in a gentler tone as he reached across the table and took her hand in his.

'Oh, Tom!' she cried. 'We have to get down to the Kirks' cottage and see her, for the poor wee thing must be in such a bad way otherwise she would have bloody walked to Glasgow to see our Robert.'

'There there now, don't you go making yourself ill over it,' he soothed. 'Just as soon as I can get away, I'll take you down to see her.'

As she waited for Tom to finish out in the byres, Ina made up a large basket of food, including butter, milk and cheese to take with them.

The staff at the Hall sat around the kitchen table talking of the events the night before.

'Oh, you should have seen the Mistress's face when she saw her man walking into the sitting room like he owned the place,' said Mary. 'And God only knows what will happen the day when the Master gets up.'

'What if he chucks us all out on our arses?' piped up Mabel.

'Don't be so bloody daft, lassie,' said Cook. 'It would be pandemonium from start to finish. Could you imagine him, or his sister for that matter, in here preparing their own food? Christ, I could just see it, they wouldn't know where to start.'

'I can't help feeling sorry for the Master though,' said Mary. 'Imagine having lived with somebody all those years and not having a clue that they were already married, and to a convicted criminal at that.'

'Aye, you never know what's in front of you all the same,' said Cook as she shook her head.

'Here, I wonder where the Mistress and Mrs. Mead ended up last night, for he tossed them out with nothing but the clothes they stood in,' said Mabel.

'God knows,' replied Cook then she laughed heartily. 'Could you just imagine her staying at the Starr Inn? The bloody village would have a field day.'

'Aye, especially if she was washing the dishes and cleaning the tables for her keep,' said Mary. 'And it serves her right, for she was nothing but a pure bitch.'

'What the hell is William going to do, what with his mother flung out the house an' all?' said Mabel.

'Aye well, I expect the minute he gets back the Master will toss him out an' all,' answered Mary, feeling very self-righteous.

Maggie and Jessie were sitting by the open door of the oven, both wrapped in thick blankets. There was no work for John today at Barr mill and he was out at the back of the cottage chopping up an old table for the fire.

'Drink your tea before it gets cold,' said Jessie, 'and don't be fretting. We've not died of the winter yet.'

Maggie smiled and said, 'I don't know what I would do without you and your da, Jessie.'

The girls fell silent as they heard voices from outside the front of the cottage. Maggie's heart lurched in her chest. She was afraid that once William Baird knew that she had survived his attack on her, he would come looking to finish her off.

Jessie quickly rose to her feet and ran to the window, but she couldn't see who was standing there talking to her father.

The next minute her father's voice seemed to stop and there followed an eerie silence, then all at once three people piled into the kitchen and it seemed that they were all talking at the same time.

It took Maggie a second or two to realize that she was looking into the face of Robert's mother as she stood over her.

'Oh my God, lassie!' Ina said, her voice shaking with emotion. She could not believe that the young girl sitting huddled in a blanket was Maggie Brown. The last time Ina Turner had seen a face so pale was on that of a dead person. The large eyes that had once sparkled like crystals were dull and sunken into their sockets, and her hair hung lifelessly over her shoulders.

John laid down the pile of wood that he had chopped and asked the Turners if they would like a mug of tea. Ten minutes later they were all sitting at the table, tucking into the basket of food that Ina had brought for them.

'How are things at the cabinet-making these days?' asked Tom.

'I've never known it to be so slow,' answered John. 'Still, I'm not afraid of a day's work; I'll make sure I get fixed up somewhere. As a matter of fact, I was hoping to get set on at the blacksmiths. I hear he's looking for a hand over the next few weeks and just as soon as he opens up the day, I'll be along there.'

Tom looked across the table at his wife, who had cupped her hands around her mug of tea to keep them warm. Even though there was a fire burning, the room felt cold and damp.

'How would you feel about giving me a hand up at Shields? What, with Robert away for the time being, it would really help me out,' said Tom.

John felt more than surprised by Tom's offer and it was on the tip of his tongue to ask if he had heard right.

'That's a grand idea,' Ina said. 'And there would be all the milk that you could drink and plenty to eat an' all,' she added for good measure.

John didn't hesitate for a second. 'Well, that would be just the job, and I don't mind getting up in the middle of the night for milking,' he added enthusiastically. To seal the new job, the men shook hands.

Then Ina came up with another idea as she said, 'It seems daft you trudging all the way up to the farm every day. It's a big place and we have more than enough room for the three of you and,' she looked at Jessie as she said, 'I really could be doing with a hand in the house if you would be good enough to work for us, Jessie?'

Jessie was beside herself. 'Oh aye, Mrs. Turner, I'll work for you and I can cook an' all.'

'Then that's it settled,' said Ina. 'Well there's no time like the present, so let's get the cart loaded up with as much as you'll need.'

Jessie couldn't help but feel sorry for her da as they loaded up the cart with their clothes and a few bits and pieces of sentimental value. She was also surprised that he was willing to shut up the cottage, even if only for a short time, for he was a proud man. But pride wouldn't feed them through the long hard winter and she knew that he was man enough to realize it.

Maggie and Ina were sitting on the cart whilst Tom was making sure the back of the cottage was secure. John stood in the kitchen and took the carriage clock down from the mantle and held it in his hands. His wife had always loved the clock that had been given to them on the day of their marriage.

He held it close to his chest as though he were cradling a new bairn.

'Come on, Da,' said Jessie, who had been watching him from the kitchen door. 'It's not for ever,' she whispered.

Malcolm and Connie sat at the breakfast table, each lost in their own thoughts. The shocking events of the previous night had left them with little appetite. For once Connie could not find any words of comfort to offer her brother, and a heavy atmosphere prevailed.

'I meant to say to you that I found something very interesting on the occasional table in the sitting room last night, once they'd gone,' said Malcolm, breaking the silence.

Connie looked up from her plate and waited for him to continue. 'Really, dear, what was it?'

It was the pendant that I'd bought for Maggie in London; just sitting there, still in its wrapper.'

Oh my God, Malcolm,' said Connie as she stood up from the table. 'We have to get the Police involved.'

Malcolm looked at his sister as she stood there, white-faced with shock. One hand lay flat on the table as if to steady her, whilst the other lay flat against her neck.

'She must have sent one of those men to kill you before you returned to Scotland.' She rounded the table and stood by her brother's side. 'And when you survived the attack,' she continued, 'they came here after you.'

'Sit down, my dear, for you look quite pale.'

Once she was seated, Malcolm continued, 'The man who found the pendant on the night of the attack was not the one who tried to murder me. The other man, her husband, did find the pendant that night and he traced her to the Hall. She must have paid her childhood friend to finish me off last night, but as luck would have it he met up with Shelly as he came to claim his wife. Now we have to get to the cottage and get Maggie.'

He rose and walked toward the door adding, 'And the sooner the better. Now hurry, my dear, we must not waste any more time.'

And he left the room with Connie following behind.

In an old wood hut in the grounds of the Hall sat Regina Shelly and her sister, Jean, huddled together under sack clothes as they tried to save themselves from freezing.

Blood, which had splattered down Regina's face from the beating she received from her husband, had dried and covered the bodice of her dress. Her lip was swollen and she could only manage to open one eye as she sat shivering in the icy refuge.

'What the hell do we do now?' asked Jean dejectedly.

'We get back into the house one way or another,' replied Regina.

'Don't be so bloody stupid!' cried Jean. 'How the hell are we going to manage that? We were tossed out on our ears last night, remember? You're not the Lady of the House any more, so we can hardly just walk in as if nothing happened. We'll be the talk of the bloody village by now an' all, so we can't show our faces there. What the hell are we going to do?'

'Will you shut up and use your head,' said Regina and threw her sister a scathing look. 'We wait here until the time is right and then we go into the house by the servants' quarters. Once there, we make our way to your office and collect the money from the safe,' she stopped talking for a moment.

A worried expression crossed her face before she said, 'Please tell me you have the keys?'

Jean lifted her skirts and in one of her petticoats there was a deep pocket from which she retrieved the keys.

'They're here,' she said, 'and I reckon there will be enough money in the safe to keep us going for years to come.'

'Oh, you think so!' snapped Regina. 'Do you really think that Jack Shelly is gone? Because if you do, then you have a very poor memory.'

Confused, Jean replied, 'But he got what he wanted and that was to see you humiliated and exposed, not to mention thrown out. Then he half-blinded you with a beating while that idiot Macey stood and watched. What the hell else can he take?'

Regina looked at her sister in sheer disgust And with venom in her voice, she said, 'He'll take whatever he wants; always has and always will.'

The sound of horses' hooves silenced the two women and, as they peered through the gaps in the wooden slats, they recognized the carriage from the Hall.

'I don't believe it!' said Jean excitedly. 'It's him and his sister off out somewhere.'

'Let me see,' said Regina as she pushed Jean out of the way so that she could get a better view of the grounds. 'By God, it is them, and by the looks of it they're going a distance.'

'Quick!' shouted Regina. 'Make for the trees and then through the side garden and into the house.'

As they ran, Regina was forming a plan in her mind and nothing was going to dissuade her. If she couldn't live out her days at the Hall, then neither would Malcolm.

Once they got as far as the side garden, they hid behind a tall hedge until they were satisfied that all was clear. Then they made a dash for the servants' door and within seconds they were inside the house. They very quickly made their way to Jean's office.

She unlocked the door, and only once they were safely inside did they realize that they had both been holding their breath. They stood behind the door and gulped at the air until their breathing returned to normal. Jean fumbled with the keys until she found the correct one for the safe and quickly unlocked it. Inside were wads of money, stolen over the years from the housekeeping allowance.

Jean piled the money into a bag as Regina stood at the window looking out onto the garden.

'Well, don't just stand there,' whispered Jean, 'give me a hand with this lot.'

She cleared the top of her desk. When Regina didn't respond, Jean stopped what she was doing and walked over to where her sister was standing.

'What's so bloody important out there?' she asked.

But when Regina turned around to face her, she had a strange look on her face and Jean became alarmed.

'What the hell's the matter with you?' she asked.

Regina walked across the room and stopped by the large fireplace before she said, 'You wouldn't understand.'

'Understand what?'

'It doesn't matter; not now. Not ever,' replied Regina.

Jean had a terrible feeling that her sister had lost her mind. She walked over so that she was face to face with her, but she stood as still as a statue looking right through her as if she was seeing something beyond the room.

'Regina!' hissed Jean, as she took hold of her sister by the shoulders and shook her. 'Get a hold of yourself or we are going to get found out, do you hear me?'

But Regina did not answer. Instead she walked to the door of the office and opened it.

Jean was flabbergasted. 'What the hell are you doing?' she whispered.

'I'm going upstairs to my room,' said Regina, as though the events of the previous night had never taken place.

Afraid that they would be spotted, Jean darted along the passageway and, before she headed out of the door, she turned to see her sister walk past the kitchen door. She's lost her bloody head, she thought, as she made her escape out into the side garden and along toward the wood hut.

Mary Fields stood with her mouth hanging open as she watched Regina Baird walk up the stairs of the Hall.

'Bloody hell!' she gasped as she ran back toward the kitchen.

When she burst into the room, Cook screamed with fright as she let the glass full of whisky fall to the floor.

'Christ, girl!' she shouted. 'What the hell's up with you, running around like a bloody clown?'

'Oh, you'll never guess who I just saw walking up the stairs?'

'Father bloody Christmas!' said Cook as she knelt down to pick up the broken glass from the floor.

'The Mistress!' cried Mary.

'Here, how many of those sherries have you had?' laughed Cook.

'I'm bloody well telling you, she just walked up the stairs.'

'Wait a minute,' said Cook, 'how many whiskies have I had? I could have sworn you said the Mistress…'

Just then Mabel Forrester burst into the kitchen and screamed at the top of her voice, 'You'll never guess who I just saw walking up the stairs?'

'Jesus Christ!' cried Cook. 'Not another one. It's a bloody double act in here the day.'

'Oh, shut it!' said Mary. 'I'm telling you, she's back in the house.'

Cook sat herself down on a chair and said, 'Did you just tell me to shut it?'

'Bloody hell, she's as drunk as a monkey,' said Mary.

Jeanie Cummings walked into the kitchen and, before she could utter a single word, both Mary and Mabel said, 'We know. She just walked up the stairs.'

Confused by what they had just said to her, Jeanie asked, 'Am I the only bugger in the house that's sober the day?'

Upstairs Regina walked around her room, lovingly touching the soft fabric of her nightgown that lay across her bed. Then she walked to the window and took hold of the crimson drape and held it to her face. She sat on the *chaise longe* and gently rocked herself backwards and forwards for some time, tears streaming down her face.

When the carriage stopped outside Thistle Cottage, Malcolm sensed that there was something very different about the look of the place.

As he and Connie reached the door, to their surprise it was thrust open by a dishevelled-looking woman who asked, 'What the hell do you want?'

Stunned, Malcolm replied, 'I wish to speak with Maggie Brown.'

Suddenly realizing who she was addressing, the woman's demeanour immediately changed. It was the talk of the village that the Laird was looking for his daughter.

'Oh, your Lordship,' she began as she suddenly bent forward in a dramatic curtsy. Her wide smile revealed a row of uneven blackened teeth, but before she could say any more her husband appeared at the door.

'Walsh is the name,' he said, offering his hand to Malcolm who ignored the courtesy. 'What can I do for you?' he said.

'You can start by telling me what you are doing in this house,' snapped Malcolm.

'Your good lady rented it to us fair and square when the old yin that lived here kicked the bucket.'

Furious, Malcolm grabbed the man by the throat and pushed him farther into the cottage. 'I will give you till the end of the day to get your brood out of this cottage and off my land,' growled Malcolm as he let go of Walsh.

The coachman jumped down from the carriage and ran up the pathway to the door.

'You heard the Laird,' he shouted as he stood between the two men.

'You can't do that!' piped up his wife.

Ignoring her statement, Malcolm shouted, 'Where is Maggie Brown?'

'She's at the Kirks' cottage, just outside the village,' said Walsh.

Without any further conversation, Malcolm turned and walked briskly back to the carriage, followed by Connie and their coachman.

When they reached the Kirks' cottage it was plain to see that the place was empty. Feeling utterly dejected, Malcolm asked the coachman to take them to Hill View House, for he couldn't contemplate returning to the Hall just yet.

Jean Mead returned to the wood hut, thinking that she would sort out the money, pack her belongings properly and wait till dark to make her next move. As she was nearing the hut, she wondered if Regina would regain her sanity and get out of the house before Malcolm returned.

The wooden door creaked as she pushed it open and suddenly she found herself face to face with Jack Shelly. She turned and made to run, only to be caught by Thomas Macey, who quickly dragged her back inside.

'Not so bloody fast!' said Macey as he struggled with her.

'You're going nowhere for the time being, so just you sit yourself down,' he added as he pushed her onto the floor.

'Take your hands off me, Thomas Macey!' cried Jean.

'Shut it,' said Shelly, 'and you can drop the lady act an' all, for we all know that you ain't a lady.'

He sat on a dusty sack filled with straw. 'Now then, you better start by telling me where Regina is. And then, we'll talk money.'

'Regina went back into the house,' she said. 'I swear to God she did; walked right up the stairs.'

'You're lying!' hissed Shelly.

'She went back into the bloody house, I'm telling you,' repeated Jean. 'Go down there and see for yourself, the Master and his sister are out.'

'What's in the bag?' he asked her.

'Keep your thieving hands off it!' she cried as she pushed the bag beneath her skirts and sat on it. But Jack Shelly wanted compensation for all the years he had been a prisoner whilst his wife lived in the lap of luxury.

He bent toward her as he said, 'I did hard time for that bitch, trying to keep her and the boy fed. Then she ups and marries a bloody gentleman, with not so much as a thought for her old man. But she didn't reckon on me coming back on the scene now, did she?'

'It's not my bloody fault what she did,' said Jean.

'But you took her handouts,' he hissed as he grabbed hold of her, hauling her up from her sitting position and throwing her into the corner.

Afraid now, for she knew how bad Jack Shelly's temper was and she didn't think for one minute that he had changed, Jean said, 'Take what you bloody want and leave me alone.'

'Oh, I intend to take exactly what I want,' he replied as he lifted the bag from the floor and handed it to Macey.

As the two men made for the door, Shelly turned around and said, 'You and your sister can rot in hell.'

The next minute they were gone and Jean was left crouched in the corner of the hut, alone and penniless.

The staff at the Hall were all gathered in the kitchen, each one wondering what to do about the Mistress's return.

'Well, I'm not bloody going up there to see to her,' said Mary Fields. 'Best to wait till the Master gets back and he can deal with her.'

'Here, what's that smell?' said Mabel.

'Jesus Christ, it's smoke!' shouted Mary.

And as they realized that the upper floor was on fire, there was a scramble for the kitchen door as they all tried to get out of the servants' quarters and into the garden.

Cook, who had fallen into a drunken sleep, sat in her chair by the fire, oblivious to the situation. When most of the staff ran into the gardens, they saw that the whole of the top floor of the Hall was engulfed in flames.

Mary Fields and Mabel Forester both ran back into the house to get Cook out of the kitchen, and found her wandering amid the dense smoke that swirled around the kitchen like a black fog.

'Jesus Christ!' shouted Cook, as the two girls each took hold of her by the arms. 'I can't have a bloody nap without you two setting fire to the oven.'

Outside on the snow-covered lawns, the staff stood and watched as the fire raged through the Hall at a tremendous speed, destroying everything in its path.

The horses were led out of the stables and put into the front field, while the State carriage was pushed far enough away from the house.

Alice Burns screamed as she pointed to an upstairs window where the glass panes were still intact. When everybody followed her gaze, it was to see the figure of Regina Baird beating at the window with her arms on fire, her screams lost in the crackling roar of the inferno.

The two stable lads, followed by the butler and three female staff members, ran from the lawns into the front field and headed for the village. The girls, screaming at the top of their lungs, shouted that the place had been cursed and if they knew what was good for them, the rest of the staff should follow and get as far away from the place as possible.

The smoke and flames could be seen for miles around and, as the carriage carrying Malcolm Baird and his sister turned round a bend in the road, they could see that the Hall was in flames.

The driver pulled the horses to a halt and Malcolm jumped down from the carriage. Stunned, he stood there watching his home burn to the ground.

'Hurry!' he addressed the coachman, who stood beside him open-mouthed, his eyes bulging. 'Get us back to the Hall as fast as you can.'

≈ 16 ≈

December 20th 1888

Cook, Mabel Forrester, Mary Fields and Jeannie Cummings were the only members of staff willing to work at Hill View House. The rest, although not harmed in the fire at Baird Hall, were determined to seek employment elsewhere for fear that the curse that was said to have reigned there would follow them to Hill View.

It had been two days since the terrible blaze at the Baird residence and all that remained of the Hall were blackened walls that stood forlornly against the grey sky.

The staff were all paid their wages and given references, and those that wished to remain in Malcolm's employ were installed in their new positions.

The remains of Regina Baird were hastily buried in the family plot with no special service.

Word of the fire had spread around most of Ayrshire, not missing Shields Farm. Maggie felt sorry for Malcolm but did not wish to convey her sympathies to him.

She was making a good recovery from her assault and, for the first time since that terrible night, she was dressed in her day clothes and sitting at the table chatting with Ina.

'I can't get over how well you look this morning,' said Ina with a wide smile on her face.

Maggie smiled back and said, 'I can't thank you and Mr. Turner enough for taking us in. I know that John and Jessie were fretting about how we would survive with very little money coming in.'

'Well, that's all behind you now,' said Ina. 'I'm just happy to see a smile on your face, and it's Tom and Ina, not Mr. and Mrs.'

Maggie blushed.

Ina went on, 'And don't forget, John and Jessie are working for their keep and doing a good job at that. It's good to see Tom perking up a bit, what with having another man around the place to moan to.' She winked at Maggie.

After their evening meal Tom and John sat quietly playing cards whilst the three women busied themselves sewing doilies and chatting about the new milliner's shop that had opened in the village.

Ina was happy to have Maggie and Lizzie's company about the place, for she sorely missed Robert. Her heart fell as she thought of him sitting in a cell while they were cosy by a warm fire.

The lawyer they had hired believed that, with the new statements from Hugh and Nelly Baxter, Robert would be a free man come New Year. But the New Year was only eight days away and, try as she might, Ina couldn't imagine her son being out of that terrible place by then.

≈ 17 ≈

Christmas Day 1888

It was three o'clock in the afternoon by the time the Christmas meal came to an end at Shields Farm. It had been a solemn affair, with few words spoken as they ate their festive fare.

'Right, let's get this lot cleared away,' said Maggie as she rose from the table.

'Aye, that's a good idea,' responded Jessie, who was glad to have something to focus on because the atmosphere was heavy.

Robert was not with them. Had he been, then the roof of the kitchen would have lifted from its rafters, with a celebration the likes of which had never been seen at the farm.

Ina was sitting quietly thinking of him and her heart ached. And then there was this business with Katy Baxter. She had not been mentioned between them, as it was as though the very sound of her name would somehow make her allegations against Robert less of a fantasy and more real than any of them could bear.

Finally she stood up from the table and said, 'I feel a bit chilled.'

She lifted her shawl from the back of her chair and wrapped it around her shoulders.

'Here, sit by the fire,' said Jessie, as she helped sit Ina down on an easy chair by the fireplace.

'Are you alright?' asked Tom, who thought that she looked a bit on the pale side.

'Don't fuss around me,' she snapped at him before adding, 'I need to be with my own thoughts for a while, that's all.'

Tom knew exactly what was ailing her, for he too felt the sadness at not having his son at home with them.

In the kitchen the girls set about washing the dishes as John and Tom stretched their legs out in the courtyard.

'I'm of a mind to visit the inn for a dram or two,' said Tom, 'but I know that you've been on the wagon for a time so…'

John interrupted him in an effort to save any embarrassment by saying, 'Get yourself down there. In fact, I'll take a walk with you as far as the Kirk.'

There was a silent understanding between the two men as they regarded each other for a moment then returned indoors to don their coats. By the time they had reached the village, Tom Turner knew a new respect for John Kirk as they parted ways.

John turned around and headed for the graveyard to visit two graves, his wife's and Lizzie Brown's. The snow had started to fall and the sky was heavy. As he ambled along, he counted his blessings.

His pride could have easily stopped him from taking the job from Tom Turner, but pride didn't feed and keep a body warm. He and Jessie did a good day's work for their pay and for that reason he felt at peace with himself.

A smile creased his face as he thought of last Christmas, when he had been so drunk that Jessie had found him sprawled across her mother's grave. He straightened his back and cleared his throat just as he arrived at his wife's resting place.

He took off his cap and held it in front of his chest and said, 'Hello, my bonny lass.'

And, as though a warm blanket had been wrapped around him, he felt a glow inside him that brought tears to his eyes.

Jack Shelly, Thomas Macey and Alex Walsh left the village inn and headed toward the disused cottage that Regina had set Macey up in whilst they were plotting Malcolm's demise.

Walsh was grateful to have a roof over his head after being evicted from Maggie's home. His wife and two daughters had gone back to her mother's house, a place where he was not welcome.

He wondered if he would be better off going back to London with his new cronies, but these men were as rough as they came and he was under no illusions about them; they could turn on him quick as a wink. No, he would bide his time with them until they were able to get a train out of Scotland.

When they reached the cottage, they were surprised to see candles lit and smoke wafting out of the chimney. Once inside, Jack Shelly came face to face with his son and, not only that, but Jean Mead sat hunched by the fire.

'Who the hell are you to just walk in here?' demanded William.

Jean's laughter sounded forced as she said, 'Well, boy, meet none other than your father, come to claim what's his.'

The look on William's face was one of sheer horror as he looked at the rough, unkempt man in utter disbelief.

'So, this is the man himself,' said Shelly as he walked farther into the room and took in the white-skinned, well dressed, pampered creature that Regina had been so proud of.

A boom of laughter escaped from deep within Shelly's gut as he looked at the horrified expression on his son's face.

'Aye, it's me, your old da, come to take you back home to London,' he said as he watched William's expression change to sheer terror.

'My God, boy, what the hell has she turned you into, with your fancy clothes and your posh accent?' said Shelly as he walked closer to his son. 'I would be ashamed to be seen with the likes of you, boy, and that's a fact.'

'Get away from me, you imbecile!' shouted William. 'You're not any father of mine.' He spat the words out. 'I refuse to believe that my mother would lower herself to look upon you, let alone lie with you.'

A crushing silence descended upon the room for a few seconds, before all hell broke loose. Jack Shelly's fist crunched straight into William's face, sending him reeling backward toward the fire where Jean was seated.

In an instant Jack was upon his son, dragging him across the floor into the middle of the room. Jean screamed and launched herself on top of William in an effort to save him from a severe beating.

With one hand, Shelly grabbed her by the hair and tossed her aside. Scrambling to her feet, she pleaded with her brother-in-law to leave the boy alone.

'It's not his fault, man,' she cried. 'It's Regina that was responsible for this mess, not him.'

When Jack Shelly turned his glare on her, she saw murder in his eyes, and by God she knew him well enough to believe exactly what he was capable of.

Fearing the worst, Jean ran from the room and hastily retrieved the bag of money from beneath a three-legged stool in the scullery that she had found earlier stuck in the chimney breast before she had lit the fire. She knew that William was in grave danger, but she could do nothing to save him, so she fled from the cottage by the back door and headed for the village.

Meantime Shelly had lifted his son from the floor by the collar of his shirt and held him close to his own face.

'You were the light of my life when you were born, boy.' His voice sounded like the growl from an injured animal, as William tried unsuccessfully to break free from the vice-like grip.

'And to think that I did years of hard labour after being caught thieving just to keep you and your mother fed, for there were no hand-outs for the likes of us, boy. Born into poverty in Whitechapel, where the lucky ones die young and the likes of me that were spared, had to fight like hell just to survive.

'And then there are the likes of you,' he spat the words out as he tightened his grip on William's collar. 'The filthy rich, pampered, good-for-nothings that look down their noses at the likes of me.'

All the rage that had built up in him over the years for the pampered life that Regina had secured for not only her, but also for this useless excuse for a man that was his son, overcame him.

In an instant he took the knife from his pocket and plunged it into William's chest. As he watched the life leave his son's eyes, he let go of him and the young man crumpled to the floor.

'Jesus Christ, man! You've done him in!' said Alex Walsh.

When Shelly looked at him, there was madness in his eyes, and Walsh too decided to leave the cottage just as soon as he could.

Jean Mead had almost reached the village when she stumbled upon an off-duty police officer and his wife, as they made their way home from their day's jollifications with friends from a nearby house.

'Oh, please help me, Sir,' she addressed the young gentleman as she grabbed hold of the sleeve of his coat.

Unbeknown to her, she told the whole sorry story to a man of the law, for she was terrified that Shelly would set out to find her.

In the hours that followed, several police officers had surrounded the cottage and all three men were escorted to the police station in nearby Beith. Jean Mead, in spite of her protests, was taken into custody with a bagful of stolen money in her possession.

The next morning, as Connie descended the stairs at Hill View House, she was surprised to see two police officers being shown into the drawing room by Mary Fields.

'What is going on, Fields?' she addressed the maid, who informed her that the Police were anxious to speak to Sir Malcolm.

'That will be all, Fields,' said Connie. 'Be good enough to return to your duties immediately.'

'Yes, Ma'am,' replied a wide-eyed Mary, as she made to return to the servants' quarters.

Knowing full well that Connie was watching her, she knew that if she ran as she was desperate to do, she may be sacked for gossiping. But she could not wait to get to the kitchen with tales of the Police wanting to speak to the Laird.

In the drawing room, Malcolm and Connie were told of the murder of William, of the stolen money, and finally, the trespassing on one of Malcolm's properties.

Before they left, one of the officers turned to Malcolm and said, 'I believe that you would find young Maggie Brown currently residing at Shields Farm, Sir.'

'Thank you,' replied Malcolm as he shook the officer's hand.

Two hours later, Malcolm and Connie stood outside the front door of the farmhouse and, as they waited for an answer to their knock, his nerves were tense.

'Who on earth could that be at the front of the house?' said Ina, for it had been a long time since anyone had knocked on that door.

'Well, you'll not know till you open it,' said Maggie with a mischievous glint in her eye.

'Somebody's on form the day,' piped up Jessie, as she stirred a pot of stew on the stove.

Ina left the smiling girls in the kitchen as she went to open the door.

As soon as she opened the door, she knew that the Laird had come to claim Maggie and she suddenly felt protective over the girl. She showed Malcolm and Connie into the sitting room and closed the door behind them, whilst she went to fetch Maggie.

Oh, dear God, she thought, as she walked along the length of the hallway back to the kitchen. How would Maggie cope with the news that she was the Laird's daughter? And would she blame her and Tom for not saying anything to her about it? But it was not their place to tell her such a thing.

As she opened the door, the two girls looked up at her expectantly and she simply said, 'You have visitors, Maggie.'

'Me?' said Maggie. 'Who on earth would visit me?'

'Well now, lass,' said Ina as she walked over to the surprised girl and gently took her in her arms and held for a moment.

'All I'm saying, lass, is for you to listen to what they have to say to you. Do you hear me now? Just hear them out before you go saying anything,' added Ina.

Feeling even more confused than before, Maggie slowly walked out of the kitchen and down the hallway to the sitting room. As she pushed the door open, she was shocked to find that Malcolm Baird, accompanied by a lady she had never seen before, standing in the middle of the room. She felt her back stiffen at the sight of Malcolm and it took all of her strength not to turn and run back.

'Maggie,' said Malcolm as he walked toward her with his arms outstretched. But, before he could reach her, Maggie swiftly moved away from him.

Realizing that this was going to be more difficult than they had anticipated, Connie stepped forward and introduced herself but Maggie did not respond.

'Why don't we sit down, my dear?' said Connie. 'I realize that you may be surprised to see us, but we have some very important information to impart to you.'

'I can't think of anything you need to say to me,' said Maggie as she looked directly at Malcolm.

Hurt at her indifference, he said, 'Maggie, my dear, all I am concerned about is your wellbeing...'

'My wellbeing?' repeated Maggie as her anger flared within her. 'Oh, you were most concerned about my welfare when you threw me out of your cottage as soon as my mother died.

'I know what you did,' she shouted. 'You used my mother in the worst way possible. You pretended to be interested in my welfare as I was growing up, when all the time you were using my mother for your own pleasure.'

Tears were rolling down her face as she went on, 'It was all a lie; every word you ever said to me was a lie.'

Stunned, Malcolm took a step backwards as he listened to his daughter's tirade.

'You made a mockery out of my childhood as you abused my mother, and your son did the same to me. I swear to God that for as long as I live, I will never again be in your company.'

As she turned to run from the room, Connie sprang to her side, blocking her exit.

'Maggie,' she said, 'whoever told you this horrible thing is lying.'

Malcolm, recovering from his shock, swiftly joined his sister by Maggie's side.

'Maggie, my child, I beg you to listen to what I have to say to you. Your mother was the most wonderful woman ever to grace this world with her presence. When she came to the village looking for work all those years ago, I fell in love with her and she with me. I insisted that she did not work at the Hall, for I wanted her to be mistress of her own home.

'She never took anything that she didn't work for and she insisted that she never would. When she found that she was having my child, I begged her to move into Hill View House and live there in luxury. But she refused.

'She refused because she could never have been a kept woman and she worked hard for her living. I had nothing but the greatest respect for her from the moment we met, and I will love her till the day I die.

'You are my daughter, Maggie, and I love you more than you could ever know. Your mother and I decided to tell you the truth of your birth when I returned from business in London, but she died before my return.'

Maggie's face grew pale and the energy left her body as she fainted into her father's arms.

≈ 18 ≈

Spring 1889

Katy Baxter had laboured for two days and was lying in her bed exhausted with the effort of pushing her child into the world.

'Come on, now,' said Annie McCaw. 'When the next pain hits you, push as hard as you can.'

'I am bloody pushing!' shouted Katy. 'Just get it out of me; pull the bloody thing out of me!'

Her next screams could be heard outside in the street as a new wave of pain ran through her body.

'I can see the head!' shouted Annie over the din. 'Push as hard as you can.'

As she did as she was told, Katy's body ripped in order to free the head from her and she screamed in agony as her child was born.

'Jesus, Mary and Joseph!' declared Annie, as she caught the child in her hands. Not only was he large, but he had carrot red hair.

'Bloody hell, I've just delivered my grandson!' cried Annie. 'I swear to God, he's the spit of our Jack. He's a big bonny lad and no mistake.'

Annie wrapped the child up in a muslin cloth and handed him to his mother.

'Get it away from me!' screamed Katy as she looked upon her son.

'What the hell are you on about?' demanded Annie. 'This is your bairn. Now take hold of him and get him onto your breast.'

'I swear to God that if you bring that thing near me, I'll toss it across the room,' cried Katy.

Nelly Baxter stood by the side of her daughter's bed and never before had she felt more like slapping her. Not for her refusal to care for her bairn, but because she couldn't believe that Katy had given birth to the spit of Jack McCaw.

'Aye,' she said now as she looked down on her daughter, 'you've done it now good and bloody proper. Who in the world would put Robert Turner's name to that wee redheaded bairn?'

Annie cradled the child in her arms as she said, 'You'll not be giving any other name to this child, for he's a McCaw. And as for you,' she neared the birthing bed, 'you are not fit to bring up a pig, never mind a wee bairn.'

Annie McCaw then left the house with her grandson in her arms.

'Well, I bloody well hope you're proud of yourself,' said Nelly Baxter, 'for as far as the whole bloody village is concerned, you will be nothing but a piece of dirt. And when Robert Turner gets out of jail the morrow, he'll be well within his rights to walk straight past the bloody door because even a blind man could see that the bairn's not his.'

'Get out!' screamed Katy. 'Get out and leave me alone.'

By the time darkness fell over the village that night, every man, woman and child knew that Katy Baxter had given birth to Jack McCaw's son. And not only that, but that she had rejected the bairn from the minute she laid eyes on him.

The staff in the kitchen of Hill View House had plenty to say regarding the whole situation.

'I always knew that Katy Baxter was a bad yin,' said Mary Fields smugly.

'By, you've changed your tune, have ye no'?' said Mabel. 'I remember the day when you thought the sun shone out of her arse.'

'Shut it, the bloody pair of you,' piped up Cook, 'and get on with peeling they tatties before I cuff yer lugs for yea.'

Aye, she thought as she sat there regarding the maids, everything is back to normal and that's for sure.

The next morning brought bright sunshine that cast a warm yellow glow across the Ayrshire lowlands. The smell of spring was in the air as Maggie and Jessie sat in the garden of Hill View House.

'Are you two going to sit there all morning?' asked John Kirk as he pushed his wheelbarrow past the girls on his way to the bottom garden.

'Aye, we just might do that,' called Jessie.

'Well, it's too bright too early, if you ask me,' answered John. 'It'll rain before the day's out and you'll be sitting there like two skinned rabbits.'

Malcolm Baird laughed out loud at John's words as he rounded the corner and joined the girls.

'Well, that's you two told,' he said jovially.

'Actually, I was wondering if you,' he addressed Maggie, 'would like to join an old man in a meander around the countryside?'

Maggie laughed at her father's antics and gladly accepted his proposal.

'Well, I'm off,' said Jessie, 'just in case you add me to your ramble. I'm as stiff as a board the day, after riding Prince halfway to Kilbirnie yesterday.'

Maggie laughed at her friend's remark. 'That will teach you a lesson about horse riding; you're supposed to lead him, not the other way round.'

Jessie looked toward Malcolm and said, 'Make sure you walk the legs off of her for she's just too smug by half the day.'

They laughed as they parted ways and Maggie took her father's arm as they walked along the garden path.

Sometime later as they stood by the side of her mother's grave, Maggie looked up on the hill where the Hall had once stood.

'It was such a beautiful house,' she said.

'Yes, I suppose it was lovely to look upon,' responded Malcolm.

'Would you ever consider restoring it?' asked Maggie.

'No, my dear,' he answered, 'for it was nothing but a curse on our family.'

As they turned to walk back through the graveyard, Maggie was staggered to see Robert Turner standing by the side of the old barn. Malcolm Baird lifted his hat in acknowledgement of the young man, before he left his daughter's side.

He had not only been instrumental in Robert's liberty, but he had arranged that the young man and his daughter should meet at this very spot.

Maggie's heart almost leapt out of her chest as she gazed in disbelief and wonder at the man she adored. She took a faltering step toward him and then she ran. Robert threw his cap down on the ground and bolted to Maggie's side and, when their bodies met, they clung so tightly to each other that they could hardly breathe.

Finally relaxing their grip of each other, but not letting go, their lips met and their tears mingled. And, as the wonder of their love swirled around them like a soft warm breeze, Malcolm stood transfixed.

He would swear to his dying day that his Lizzie was standing beside them.